TALL TALES

With a Twist

Expect the unexpected

Michael Church

Tall Tales - With a Twist

ISBN: 978-1-7397937-1-5

Publisher: Bookendz

Contents

Don't Count Your Chickens

Lee Cormack stood in front of his wife, Sarah, holding some flowers.

'You didn't think I'd forget today is your birthday, did you?' he said. 'Though I feel it could be tinged with sadness as I have something to tell you. I know the timing could have been better but I feel you really should know I've met somebody else. It would mean so much to me, if you were able to give me your blessing. The thing is, I've been so unhappy for a long time, since…well, you know. And now I have a chance of regaining the happiness, I once had, with somebody else. Her name is Tiggy, but there are complications, though – she's married. Yes, I know it's wrong but I can't help who I fall in love with, can I? She works for one of the firms I deal with, that's how we met.

'There will always be a special place for you in my heart and I'll never forget you – how could I? I wouldn't want to. And I will still come to see you, I don't want to erase those happy memories I have of our time together. But I feel now is the time for me to move on – make a fresh start – and make some new memories. Yes, I know this is a betrayal on my part, and the guilt weighs heavy, believe me. But, in your heart of hearts, would you really deny me this chance of happiness?'

A tear rolled down Lee's cheek as mixed emotions coursed through him. He still loved his wife, of course he did.

'I'm sorry. This is harder than I thought it would be, but I had to tell you. Maybe you knew anyway, but I felt it was the right thing to do to actually say the words – to make it somehow honourable. Please don't judge me too harshly, I'm trying to do the right thing, I hope you can see that.'

Lee's voice was quavering. He was swallowing rapidly to hold down the raw emotion threatening to engulf him. 'I have to go now before I go to pieces. There is so much more I wanted to say. I'm sorry. Sleep tight my angel.' And, with that, he placed the flowers against the headstone and walked away, convulsed with tears.

* * *

It was a bright, sunny morning, which found Lee driving his BMW M3 through the city towards the Burnside

Industrial Estate, situated on the outskirts. A journey he had made many times in connection with his work and today was no different. It was great to get back, once again, into the groove. He had shaken off the melancholy which had pervaded following his visit to the cemetery yesterday. It felt good to be alive. The cataclysmic effects of his wife's death no longer wrenched at the sinews of his heart. That's not to say he didn't think about her. The thoughts and memories were still there, but time had dulled the pain and heartache. A new horizon had dawned for him, bringing hope and light into the darkness of the recent past.

Lee pulled into the carpark of Aztec Precision Engineering, grabbed the tube off the back seat and headed for reception. As he entered, the receptionist was talking on the phone and a man stood waiting in front of her desk. Lee stood and waited patiently, he wasn't in any particular hurry. His mind wandered to the coming evening and the delights it may have in store. Tiggy was coming over to see him and he was full of joyful expectation. It was his first relationship since the death of his wife two years ago. Life was beginning to feel good again and worth living.

'Yes, okay. If you mark it for his attention, it will reach him. Yes, that's right. Thank you for calling. Bye.'

The receptionist looked up to the man who had been waiting and said, 'Sorry about that. How can I help you?'

'I have an appointment with Mr Withers at 10 o'clock.'

'What name is it?'

'Brady. George Brady.'

'Okay, I'll let him know you're here, Mr Brady. Please take a seat.'

Lee approached the desk and looked at the attractive woman sitting there as she made the call to Mr Withers. Her lustrous, loosely curled locks of red hair cascaded down past her shoulders. The sparkle in her blue eyes was enhanced by the freckles on her cheeks and nose. She looked up at him and her smile lit up her face. It gave Lee a nice warm feeling as he reciprocated.

'Mr Withers will be with you shortly,' she said to the other man, before turning to Lee and saying, 'Hello. This is a pleasant surprise. I take it you're here to see David?'

'As ever. I've got to go through these drawings with him,' he said, waving the tube.

She picked up the phone once again, and said, 'Hello, David. Lee from Cormack Engineering Solutions is here to see you…Yes, okay, I'll do that.' and she replaced the receiver. 'David said you can go on through.'

'Thanks,' said Lee. And they maintained a lingering eye contact until he disappeared through the door.

An hour later, Lee reappeared to find the reception area empty, save for the receptionist.

'All done?' she asked.

'Yeah.'

'Sorry about earlier, I couldn't really talk to you with that other man there. Are we still on for tonight?'

'I sincerely hope so, Tiggy. What time can I expect you?'

'Oh, round about seven-thirtyish? By the time I've got home and cooked his lordship's dinner, then showered and changed.'

'Okay, I'll see you then. Take care,' and with that, he was gone.

'So, what excuse have you used for this evening?' asked Lee, as they sat enjoying a glass of wine in his lounge.

'I told Richard I was coming here to see my friend, Sarah.'

'Yeah, I'm not entirely comfortable with you using my wife's name.'

'I know, but it's best to stick as close to the truth as possible. If he was to phone to see if I was here, you would be legitimately answering as Sarah's husband and you could pass the phone to me. You could also say I've left for home, or that I had gone out with Sarah. Simple, it's fool-proof. And, being a postman, he could easily check to see if a Mr and Mrs Cormack lived here.'

Lee would have liked her to move in with him, and put the relationship on a firmer footing. But he wasn't going to put pressure on her to do so, as it was still relatively early days, and he knew he needed to take things steady.

'I suppose it makes sense. You've got it all worked out, haven't you?'

'An old head on young shoulders,' said Tiggy.

'What do you mean: "young shoulders"?'

'Excuse me! What are you trying to say? I'll have you know, I'm younger than you.'

'Not by much, you're not. How old are you, anyway?'

'How old do you think I am?'

'Oh, no. I'm not going there. That's a dangerous game to play where ladies are concerned.'

'Well, it's my birthday next week and it's a big one.'

'Really?' said Lee, genuinely surprised. 'Are you telling me you've reached the big four-O?'

'I'm afraid so.'

'I have to say, you certainly don't look it. Well, we must celebrate – what would you like to do? Ideally, I would have liked to take you away for the weekend, but I suppose that's out of the question?'

'It is, unfortunately. If only. As much as I want to, I won't be able to celebrate with you on the day. Richard would expect me to celebrate with him. He might even have something planned, so it's difficult.'

'Okay. So how about we take a day off work and I'll take you shopping to get you something nice, followed by dinner at a nice restaurant and then perhaps go to the theatre or something?'

'Oh, that would be lovely. I'd like that very much, thank you,' said Tiggy.

'So, when is your birthday?'

'Friday.'

'And what day would you like to go? Assuming you can get the day off, that is.'

'Tuesday would suit me better,' she said, 'if that's okay with you? I should be able to get the day off – I'm owed.'

'Good. Tuesday it is, then. Now let's have a look to see what's on at the theatre.'

* * *

'Did you hear what I just said?' asked Tiggy.

'Er, no. Sorry love, I was just looking at the runners and riders.'

'Typical. You're more interested in horses than you are in me. I could be having an extra-marital affair and you'd be none the wiser, would you?'

'Don't be so daft,' said Richard. 'Who else would have you?'

'You'd be surprised. I said, Sarah and I are taking the day off work on Tuesday to go shopping. She wants to buy me something for my birthday, and then we are going to the theatre in the evening. I expect you'd forgotten all about my special birthday, hadn't you?'

'Who me? No, no, of course I hadn't. Actually, I was

going to suggest taking you shopping myself so you could choose something you really like.'

'Talk about thinking on your feet,' muttered Tiggy.

'What was that?'

'Nothing. I just said, it would be different if I had four feet.'

'What would?'

'Oh, it doesn't matter. Yes, I would like you to take me shopping. Would you be able to fit it in between races, do you think?'

'Oh, come on, Tiggy, there's no need for that. Look, I've booked a day off for Friday so I can celebrate with you. I'll see if I can take the Thursday as well, and then we can hit the shops. How does that sound?'

'In theory, it's a plan, but I know what you're like when you go shopping, it's: *"Have you seen the price of that?" "How much?" "What a rip-off" "They must be having a laugh"*. I've heard it all before. You take all the joy out of shopping. You're a miserly old skinflint.'

'That's a bit harsh,' said Richard. 'I'm just careful with what little money I do have.'

'So careful, that you waste most of it on three-legged donkeys. Honestly, do you have any idea how much you spend on the horses?'

'Now, now. Seeing as it's a special birthday, I'll let you choose whatever you like and I won't complain because you're worth every penny.'

'I'm sure that I am, but the big question is, have you got enough pennies to match what I'm worth?'

'I will have,' he said, with a degree of certainty that made Tiggy a bit querulous, but she let it go.

* * *

Tiggy was at work behind the reception desk when the phone rang.

'Good morning. Aztec Precision Engineering. How may I help?'

A strange, man's voice said, 'Oh, good morning. I wonder if you could help me. Could I possibly speak to someone about left-handed screwdrivers, please?'

Tiggy paused as she thought about it, then said, 'Oh, piss off, Lee. You'll have to get up earlier than that if you want to catch me out.'

'You had to think about it, though. I take it there's no one in reception, then?'

'Correct.'

'I'm just ringing to make arrangements for our day out tomorrow. Would you like me to pick you up, or do you want to come to mine and we go from there? Alternatively, we could meet up in town. The choice is yours.'

'I think it's best if we meet up in town. What about near the fountain in Lion Square, say ten-thirty?'

'Yep. Okay. I'm fine with that. Have you given any thought as to what you would like?'

'I have given it some thought…'

'And?'

'And I haven't a clue.'

'If you had a little idea of the sort of thing you'd like, it would help to narrow down the search, rather than wandering aimlessly from shop to shop.'

'Yes, okay, it makes sense,' said Tiggy. 'Leave it with me and I'll give it some more thought. Right, I've got to go, there's somebody heading in my direction. See you tomorrow. Bye.'

* * *

It was yet another fine, September morning as Tiggy made her way to Lion Square. As she rounded the corner, she looked across to the fountain and saw Lee perched on the surrounding wall, wearing navy chinos and a pale blue jacket. He made her heart skip a beat. She couldn't help thinking how handsome he was. His tanned features lit up as he spotted her heading towards him.

'Hello, gorgeous.'

'Hello, gorgeous, yourself,' replied Tiggy, with a warm smile.

'Did you want to get a coffee before we start? We've got all day.'

'Sounds good to me. How about that place over there, across the way?'

'Okay, let's go.'

Over coffee, Lee asked her again if she'd had any more thoughts about what she might like.

'I've thought long and hard, and I still haven't got a clue.'

'What about a new outfit?'

'I don't think so. As it's a milestone, I would like something I can keep forever to remember the day – it's special, isn't it?'

'Yes, you're right. Maybe I could buy you the Koh-i-Noor diamond, that should do the trick.'

'What's that?'

'It's a famous diamond of over one hundred carats. It was presented to Queen Victoria in 1849, I believe. It's now kept in The Tower of London as part of the crown jewels.'

'Oh, so I take it it's out of the question, then?'

'I guess so, but there's nothing to say you couldn't have something a bit smaller.'

'Really?' said Tiggy, her eyes opening wide. 'Maybe that's what I could have – a small piece of jewellery.'

'Right, that's settled, then. Let's hit the jewellery shops.'

They looked in several shops but Tiggy didn't see anything which caught her eye.

'Are you looking for anything in particular?' said Lee.

'A ring, or a bracelet, perhaps?'

'I'm sorry, I don't really know, but I will do when I see it.'

'Okay, so let's go and have a look in J T Samson, they have a good selection to choose from.'

They had been looking in Samson's window for a few minutes when Tiggy said, 'Look. Look there. There's a beautiful necklace. Can you see it? It's got a beautiful pink stone.'

'Oh, yes, I can see it. It's quite eye-catching. Let's go in and have a proper look, shall we?'

'Good afternoon, Sir. Madam. Can I be of any assistance?'

'Yes,' said Lee. 'We'd like to have a look at the necklace you've got in the window.'

'The one with the pink stone,' chirped Tiggy.

'I know the one you mean. Just a moment and I'll get it for you.'

Tiggy beamed a big smile at Lee as she waited to get a close-up of the necklace.

'Here we are. It's a really fine piece of jewellery. It's got an eighteen-carat, white gold setting and chain. The teardrop pendant has a two-carat pink sapphire surrounded by one-point-one carats of diamonds.'

'Oh my god,' said Tiggy. 'It's absolutely exquisite.' She couldn't take her eyes off it.

'May I ask if it's for a special occasion?' said the

jeweller.

'Yes,' said Tiggy. 'It's a special birthday.'

'How wonderful. In that case this is perfect for Madam. The sapphire is the birthstone for September, and it's also known as the stone of passion.'

'Wow!' said Tiggy. 'It's perfect in every way. It was meant to be.'

'Would Madam like to try it on?'

'Oh, yes please.'

'If you'd just like to turn around. There we go. Let's have a look.'

Tiggy slowly turned around and the two men were both smiling, giving it their seal of approval.

'If I may say so, it was made for Madam. It matches your colouring. Have a look in the mirror – see for yourself.'

'It's absolutely fabulous,' said Tiggy. 'What do you think, Lee?'

'I think it's perfect, and you've quite clearly fallen in love with it, so it's yours.'

'Oh, thank you. Thank you. I shall be eternally grateful,' she said, giving him a kiss.

'What's the price?' said Lee.

'It's £3,250 Sir.'

Tiggy gave Lee a searching look.

'What? What's the matter?'

'I need a word,' she said, moving away from the

jeweller.

'What's up?'

In hushed tones, Tiggy said, 'I can't accept it.'

'Why not? I can afford it.'

'It's not that.'

'Then what?'

'I can't explain away to my husband how I came to have a three-grand necklace.'

'Oh, I see what you mean. We need to give this some careful thought.'

'As much as I want it, I can't see a way round the problem.'

'There must be a way,' said Lee. 'We need to think.'

'Is there a problem, Sir. Madam?'

'Er, yes, there is, a bit.'

'We can offer you terms, should you want to spread the cost.'

'No. No, it's not that. We need to go away and think about it. Tiggy, you'll have to take the necklace off for now. But we'll be back.'

Half-an-hour later, they were sitting on a bench in Tower Gardens trying to come up with a solution. Tiggy was despondent: her heart was set on having the necklace but there was, seemingly, no way of overcoming the problem. They were going over the same old ground time after time. Tiggy could have left the necklace at Lee's and wear it when she was with him, but that wasn't very satisfactory from her point of view. It screamed to be shown off, not worn in secret. And so, the rumination went on.

Suddenly, Lee said, 'Yes, I think I might just have the answer!'

'What?'

'We have to go back to the shop. I need to talk to the jeweller on a man-to-man level.'

'What do you mean?'

'Bear with me. All will be explained when we go back.'

'But you can't possibly have a way round the problem.'

'Trust me,' said Lee, with an air of confidence.

When they entered Samson's, the jeweller had a welcoming smile for them. 'Hello, it's nice to see you again. I had a feeling you'd be back, as Madam had fallen in love with it. Is everything okay? Have you managed to resolve the problem regarding the necklace?'

'Well, it rather depends on you,' said Lee.

'Naturally, I'll do whatever I can to help, if it's within my means.'

'I need to talk to you as a man-of-the-world.'

'Oh, okay. Go ahead.'

'Well, the truth of the matter is: the lady is married and I'm not her husband. So, she would have a problem trying to explain how she came to have the necklace.'

'Oh, I can see how that would be a problem, but how could I possibly be of assistance?'

'This is my proposal: I pay you the £3,250 for the necklace.'

'Yes.'

'You then hold on to the necklace until the lady comes back with her husband. You do not let on that you know her. She will *"choose"* the necklace for her husband to buy. He does not have the money to buy it, so you tell him it's paste and quote him a figure which reflects that. So, he goes away with the necklace thinking he has bought it. And you get to keep the money he gives you as a bonus for going along with my plan. How does that sound? Do we have a deal?'

'Well, it's highly irregular, Sir, but I saw for myself how much the lady likes it and I do like to know the jewellery I sell is going to someone who appreciates it. So, I suppose I could go along with it – yes.'

'Good man. Is that alright with you Tiggy?'

'Of course. It's a brilliant idea. How on earth did you come up with that?'

Lee gave her a wink by way of an answer.

* * *

'What time did you get in last night?' said Richard.

'Oh, about ten-thirty, I think. It was good of you to wait up for me,' replied Tiggy, sarcastically.

'I can't sit up half the night waiting for you; some of us have to get up early for work, you know.'

'Early to pick the horses, more like.'

'You'll change your tune when you see what I'll be able to buy you for your birthday.'

'What, six-penneth of sherbet dabs?'

'Mock all you like – you'll soon find out tomorrow.'

'You managed to get the day off, then, did you?'

'Yes, have you any ideas as to what you'd like?'

'No, not really. Something expensive I would have thought.'

'What did Sarah buy you yesterday?'

'Nothing in the end. I didn't see anything I liked which was reasonably priced.'

'See. That's exactly what I was saying the other day. These shops charge exorbitant prices.'

'What I meant was: there was nothing I fancied for what I could reasonably expect a friend to pay.'

'Oh, I see. Well, things will be different tomorrow.'

'No doubt,' said Tiggy, who had heard it all before.

* * *

'RICHARD! Come on. It's time you were getting up if you're taking me shopping.'

'Alright. I'm coming. I'm coming.'

It was nearly ten o'clock when Richard finally came down the stairs. He plonked himself down at the table with his copy of the Racing Post.

'What's for breakfast?' he said.

'Whatever you can find; I had mine hours ago.'

'Oh, come on, don't be like that. Let's not start the day off on the wrong foot. We're going to have a nice day.'

'All you'll get at this time of day is cereal and toast.'

'That would be lovely, thank you. And while you're at it, stick the kettle on, love.'

Richard sat there having his breakfast with his nose stuck in the Racing Post, whilst his wife sat impatiently waiting to go and pick up her necklace. Tiggy couldn't help wondering why she bothered. Richard had long since been the man she married all those years ago. He took her for granted and showed little interest in her. There was no longer a spark between them. Was it any wonder she was having an affair? Lee was the complete opposite, he was kind, thoughtful and attentive. He made her feel alive.

'How much longer are you going to be? At this rate the shops will be closed by the time we get there, or is that your plan?'

'Plenty of time. Plenty of time. Well, maybe not. Look, I've got a bit of business to attend to first, so—'

'Would that be with a Mr Joe Coral, or a Mr William Hill?' cut in Tiggy.

Ignoring her, Richard said, 'What I was going to say was, to save time, why don't you go into town and see if you can find yourself something. Then I'll meet up with you after I've done what I've got to do and we can then go and get it?'

'You're unbelievable, do you know that? You never really wanted to go in the first place, did you? Meet me at two o'clock in front of the fountain in Lion Square, and don't you dare be late.' With that, Tiggy stormed out of the house.

Richard sat open mouthed, oblivious to what that was all about. It wasn't as if she wasn't going to get a present. He was just trying to be helpful and constructive.

Tiggy enjoyed a lingering lunch at a bistro to pass the time. After all, she didn't need to traipse round the shops, she knew what she was going to get. And, to be honest, she'd had enough of looking in shops the other day. So it was in eager anticipation that Tiggy sauntered along to Lion Square; the necklace almost in her grasp.

'You managed to drag yourself here, then, I see.'

'There's no need to be like that. I told you I'd be here.'

'I trust your *"bit of business"* was successful, and that I shall reap the benefit,' said Tiggy.

'Well, er, have you seen anything you like?' said Richard, deflecting the question.

'No, not really, but there are a couple of streets I haven't been down yet.'

'Okay, so let's start with those, shall we?'

'I'd like something I can keep forever. Something that won't go out of fashion. Something classy and classic,' she said.

'And how much is that going to cost, I wonder?'

'I seem to recall someone saying I'd be surprised by what they would buy me.'

'Ah...well, yes, but within reason.'

'Since when have you been reasonable?'

'You need to find something first, and, when you do, that will be the time to have this discussion.'

For half-an-hour, as they went from shop to shop, Tiggy kept up the pretence of looking for something. All the time, she was trying to figure out how she could get her husband into the jeweller's. As they walked along, they eventually came to Samson's and Tiggy stopped to look in the window.

'Did you know Richard Burton once bought Elizabeth Taylor a diamond for one million pounds?' said Tiggy.

'In that case, there's no reason why you can't have one, too.'

'Very funny.'

'Come on, let's go inside and have a look,' said Richard.

'What? Are you serious?'

'Yes, why not? Obviously, I can't compete with that other Richard but there might be something I can afford.'

My god, this is going to be easier than I thought, she mused.

When they went in, the jeweller smiled at Tiggy but gave nothing away. 'Can I be of assistance? Is there anything you're particularly looking for?' he said.

'No,' said Richard. We are looking for something for my wife's birthday tomorrow. We'll just look around if that's alright?'

'But of course, Sir. If you need any help just let me know.'

As they looked around, Tiggy said, 'There are some really lovely pieces, aren't there?'

'And some really nice prices, no doubt. Is there anything you like?'

'I quite like that necklace there but it's probably too expensive.'

'We can always ask, that doesn't cost anything – I hope.'

They looked round at the jeweller. 'Have you found something?' he said.

'Yes, we'd like to have a closer look at that necklace there, please.'

'Certainly, Sir. I'll get it for you.'

When she had a closer look, Tiggy said, 'I don't know. I'm not sure.'

'How much is it?' ventured Richard.

'This particular piece is £1,249.'

Richard nearly choked as he looked at Tiggy with wide open eyes. 'How much? Have you not got anything cheaper?'

'Richard!' said Tiggy.

'It's quite alright, Madam, I understand.' Reaching behind him, the jeweller brought out *the* necklace. 'I have this teardrop pendant, Sir. It's really quite exquisite looking.'

'Oh, that's it,' said Tiggy. 'That's the one. It's absolutely fabulous. I love it. I really, really would like to have it. I wouldn't care if you never bought me anything else.'

'Steady on, love,' said Richard. 'It looks far more expensive than the other one.'

'But it's gorgeous.'

'Look, I didn't do so well on the gee-gees,' he whispered. 'In fact, they let me down.'

'How could you?' she said, through clenched teeth. 'It's my fortieth birthday!'

The jeweller cleared his throat. 'This, Sir, is paste.'

'Paste?'

'Yes, Sir. Basically, it's polished glass.'

'Oh, so does that mean…'

'Yes, Sir. It's nowhere near as expensive as the real thing.'

Richard didn't look too convinced. 'So how much would it be, then?'

'A modest £125.'

'Does that mean I can have it?' asked Tiggy, eagerly.

'Uh…Yes, I guess it does. But I haven't got enough money on me to pay for it.'

'That's not a problem, Sir. I can hold it for you for twenty-four hours if you come back with the money.'

'Yes, okay, it's not a problem.'

'Oh, thank you, Richard,' said Tiggy, flinging her arms around him. 'That's the best present ever.'

Yes, she had pulled it off. The necklace was hers.

* * *

It was lunchtime on Tiggy's birthday and her husband should have been back ages ago, having gone to collect her longed-for necklace. She felt like an excited child on Christmas Eve waiting for Santa's visit. To think they had pulled it off against all the odds, was unbelievable. Lee was a genius. Tiggy was on tenterhooks, constantly checking the time and looking out of the window to see if Richard was in sight.

'God, this is ridiculous,' she said to herself. 'You're a grown woman – get a grip.'

It was getting on for one-thirty when the errant husband, in question, returned.

'Wherever have you been? Did you get it? Where's my necklace? I've been worried something might have happened.'

'Sorry, O pretty one. I bumped into Eric and we went to the pub for a quick one.'

'One?'

'Well, alright, two…maybe three,'

'Did you get my necklace? Where is it?'

'Whoa, whoa. Steady on old girl. Slow down.'

'Don't you dare tell me you haven't got it.'

'I have, or at least I did have.'

'Did have? Where the hell is it?'

'Calm down, dear. It's all good news.'

'It doesn't sound like it to me!' she blazed.

'Listen. Just listen to me. I was long overdue a change of luck. It had to happen and today was the day!'

'What are you saying?' asked Tiggy, with a sense of foreboding.

'Look, it's okay, everything has worked out just fine. I was showing the necklace to Eric and Mike, the landlord. Mike really took a shine to it and wanted to buy it for his wife. You'll never believe it, but the fool actually offered me five-hundred quid for it. What about that? I'm quids in. Now I can take you back and buy you something better!'

'Noooooooo!'

A Secret Too Many

'Oh, it's just possible you may have saved my life.'

The lift engineer looked round to see an attractive, blonde-haired woman in her early forties, laden with several bags of shopping. 'Really? How did I manage that?'

'Have you fixed the lift? I really can't face all those stairs carrying this lot.'

'Here, let me help you with those,' he said, taking hold of some of her bags. 'It should be all right now; let's give it a test run.' They entered the lift and the engineer put down the bags. 'Which level?'

'My apartment is on the top floor.'

He pressed the corresponding button. 'Right, I can see now why the stairs would have been a problem for you.'

'It's the third time this month it has broken down, and it's no joke when you live at the top of the building.'

'Well, it is quite old but it seems to be working okay now. Third time lucky, eh?'

The lift stopped at level eight and the doors opened. 'I'll carry these to your door,' said the man, picking up her bags. 'Lead on mistress.'

'Why, thank you, kind sir,' she said, with a beaming smile. 'I'm Sasha, by the way.'

'What a lovely name, it suits you. They call me Lenny. Lenny the Lift; for more than the obvious reason.'

'How intriguing. What might that be?'

'What, the obvious reason?'

'No, silly. The other reason.'

'Aha…' said Lenny, tapping the side of his nose with his finger. 'Classified information.'

'Oh, I love a man of mystery, but right now I've got a mystery of my own, I don't know what I've done with my keys. I'm sure they were here in my handbag.'

'You women and your handbags; I'm sure you don't need half the stuff you carry around in them.'

'Got them!' said Sasha triumphantly, as she pulled them out of her cavernous bag. 'I'm absolutely gasping; would you like to come in for a drink?'

'I don't need asking twice.'

Lenny followed her into her grand, late Victorian apartment. He looked around the spacious room, the plush, draped curtains gave a feeling of warmth and opulence.

'Just put the bags down there,' she said, indicating a space between an escritoire and a bookcase.

'What's that wooden stick thing poking out of your bag?' said Lenny.

'Oh, that,' she said, pulling it out and smacking it into the palm of her hand, 'is a Polynesian tribal fighting club. It's quite heavy; the bulbous end could cause some serious damage if you happened to be on the receiving end. I picked it up from a junk shop, I thought it was a bit quirky and rather tactile. Now, what would you like to drink, tea, coffee or…?'

'Or…?'

'Well, I'm having wine but there's whisky, gin, vodka; I don't think I've got any beer.'

'Okay, I'll have a glass of wine with you, if that's all right.'

'Great. Take a seat and I'll open a bottle.'

Lenny eased himself into an oxblood Chesterfield chair as Sasha disappeared into the kitchen. I could get used to living in a place like this, he thought to himself.

'Red or white?' came from the kitchen.

'Either; I don't mind,' was the reply.

'Red it is then,' said Sasha, returning with two glasses and a bottle.

'It's a nice place you've got here, have you been here long?'

'Only a couple of years. I bought it with the inheritance

I received from my mother, otherwise I would never have been able to afford it. As it was, I only just managed to scrape together enough after paying inheritance tax.'

'I noticed you said *"I"*, do you not have a husband or partner?'

'No, not any more. He cleared off years ago. I'm quite happy on my own, I have plenty of friends.'

'It's not everyone who can say they're happy and contented.'

'Can you?' said Sasha.

'Well…reasonably, I suppose. I like my job; I don't have my boss breathing down my neck all the time. However, I'm always looking for ways to…er "supplement my income".'

'And how do you do that?'

'Oh, you know, a bit of wheeling and dealing.'

Sasha looked at the man sitting opposite her. She guessed he was probably early fifties. His swarthy, rugged looks highlighted the laughter lines radiating from his brown eyes. Yet, those eyes seemed to contain a darkness within. 'Do you have a family?'

'Yes, I've got a wife and four children to support, though two of them are at uni, but, nonetheless, I still have to support them.'

'It's no wonder you need extra money,' said Sasha. 'Here, let me top up your glass.'

'It's not a bad drop of wine,' said Lenny, holding out

his glass.

'It's only a Cotes de Rhone I picked up from the supermarket; it's nothing special.'

'Well, it's nice all the same. Tell me, how do you pay your bills?'

'I have three hair and beauty salons.'

'Wow. I'm impressed. Of course, you obviously have no need for your own services.'

Sasha smiled at that. 'Flattery will get you everywhere,' she said.

'So, how come you're not at work today?'

'I only do two days a week, unless I'm providing cover for one of the salons. I have a manager in each, so there's no need for me to be there.'

'Nice work if you can get it, I suppose. So how do you spend your time away from work?'

'Good question. The days seem to pass by quite effortlessly. I'll have a day's shopping with a girlfriend, as I did today. Sometimes I'll get out of the city and go for a drive in the country, find some rural antique shop to browse, and a country pub for lunch – a perfect day. I also like to go to auctions; you can sometimes pick up a bargain. I'm always on the lookout for something for the apartment, or to add to my collection.'

'You are very fortunate, in that, you're able to live the life you choose. Most of us are far too busy trying to keep our heads above water in order to survive. We have neither the time nor the resources to be able to follow our dreams.'

'I'll have you know, I worked bloody hard to build up my business, and I had to make sacrifices along the way to do so,' railed Sasha.

'Sorry, it wasn't meant as a criticism. I was merely saying, most people are not in a position to risk a change of direction. They have too many commitments; it's only later in life, when the mortgage is paid off and the children have fled the nest, that they are in a position to try something different. Not everybody knows what they want from life at the outset. Some only know having had a lifetime of experiences and, by then, it can be too late.'

'Yes, okay, I see what you mean. But there are people who do have a complete change of life, swapping the daily grind of a monotonous job in the city for a tranquil life raising lesser ridge-backed marmosets on some remote Hebridean island,' said Sasha.

'I really admire those people for having the courage to make that leap of faith, not knowing if it will work out. There is so much pressure attached to modern-day life – and to what ends? To maintain the expectation of a peer-led consumerism where success is measured in terms of what you own and how expensive it is. Few people appreciate the simple things in life and how beneficial they are to our wellbeing.'

'That's very philosophical for a Tuesday afternoon,'

said Sasha, the smile returning to her face. 'I think there's just about enough left in this bottle for us to have another. Hold out your glass.'

'It's a good thing I haven't got any more jobs for today: I shall be Brahms and Liszt at this rate.'

'Don't you mean Brahms and Lifts?' she giggled.

'Very droll.'

'Sorry, I'm feeling a bit squiffy. I had a couple at lunchtime, but, hey, who's counting?'

As she took a sip of wine, her sparkling eyes peered over the rim of the glass at Lenny as he, in turn, took in the vision seated opposite.

The loose curls of Sasha's hair cascaded past her shoulders onto her blue, silk blouse, which matched her eyes. He couldn't help liking what he saw, but would she be interested in him? Probably not.

'So, tell me about this top secret, mysterious side of you,' continued Sasha.

'Oh, no. I couldn't possibly tell you; if I did, I'd have to kill you.'

'It can't be that bad, can it?'

'You'd be surprised.'

'Oh, go on, surprise me. I've got a secret that would surprise you,' she said tantalizingly.

'You're not going to get me to open up that way, missy.'

'Well, I'm just going to have to ply you with drinks

until your tongue loosens up a bit. I have ways of making you talk.'

'Here's to the challenge.' Lenny raised his glass then knocked it back in one.

'You're not an alkie, are you? Is that your secret?' she said in mock horror. If that's the case, I had better get you another drink. What would you like, a drop of the hard stuff? I've got a nice bottle of 15-year-old Cardhu, single malt.'

'That would do very nicely, thank you.'

'Right, Cardhu it is,' said Sasha, standing up and draining her glass. 'I think I'll have a gin and tonic. I can't have you drinking on your own.'

She walked over to the chinoiserie drinks cabinet and opened the doors, then proceeded to pour the drinks.

'Is that an 18th century cabinet?'

'Only in style. It's a Victorian reproduction. Do you know about antiques, then?'

'A bit. I do have an interest. I always watch the Antiques Roadshow and Flog It! It's fascinating what you pick up from watching them, and I also have the odd book or two.'

'Sounds like you're really into antiques; are you a collector?'

'I've got a few bits and pieces, but I can't afford the one's I really like,' said Lenny.

'Yes, I know what you mean. I have the same problem

too, but there is a way around it.'

'Oh, yes. What's that?'

It was Sasha's turn to tap her nose with her finger.

'Touché!' said Lenny with a smile, as he took the proffered glass.

'Want to trade?' said Sasha.

'No. I told you, I couldn't possibly divulge my secret.'

'You had better keep drinking then.'

'You're a very determined lady, aren't you?'

'Yes, I usually get what I want in the end.'

'I notice you've got a few nice pieces of porcelain. Is that Worcester?' he said, looking at a vase on a small console table.

'Correct. I do like decorative porcelain but my main interest is in silver, as you can see from my collection in that glass cabinet.'

Lenny got up and wandered over to the cabinet. 'It's quite a collection you've got here, and there's a few unusual pieces. It must have taken you a long time to acquire them.'

'Yes, I've built up the collection over the past ten to fifteen years. I pick up pieces here and there on my travels, and some are gifts.'

'They must take a lot of cleaning.'

'You're not supposed to polish them too often because you can wear away the silver and lose some of the fine detail.'

'Oh, I see. I must remember that.'

'Do you have some silver then?'

'Only the one piece which I—.' Lenny just managed to check himself before it slipped out.

'Which you…?'

'No…nothing. It's nothing – really.'

'Methinks it's time you had another drink,' said Sasha mischievously, sensing his guard was beginning to slip. 'Same again, is it?'

'Thank you, I don't mind if I do.' Lenny returned to his seat as Sasha poured him another generous measure of whisky.

'There you go, get that down you.'

'I could get used to drinking this,' he said, taking a sip. 'What more could you ask for? Lovely apartment, lovely company and a drink of pure nectar. It couldn't be more relaxing.'

Suddenly there was a knock on the door.

'Who can that be?' said Sasha.

'There's only one way to find out.'

Sasha went to the door and opened it.

'Hiya Sash, how you doin'? I've got something I think you'll be interested in.'

'Oh, hello Jake. Er, now's not a good time.'

'It's the only time I've got. There's somebody else who would want it, but I'm giving you first refusal as you're a good customer who appreciates what I have to offer.'

'Well, er…' She looked round at Lenny, who smiled at her.

'Don't mind me,' he said, 'you just carry on as if I wasn't here.'

'Oh, I didn't realize you had company,' said Jake. 'Is it okay?'

Sasha looked nervously between the two men, not sure what to do. She was clearly embarrassed. 'I don't know, I mean, er…okay, what the hell. Come in. What have you got this time?'

'You'll love it. It's in mint condition,' said Jake putting his hand inside a bag. 'Look, a silver chamber candlestick holder, complete with sconce, and it's even got the snuffer as well. You won't get better than that.'

Sasha held it in her hands and her eyes lit up as she examined it – it was exquisite. She looked at the hallmarks and saw the initials RG. 'It's Garrard, isn't it?'

'Sure is.'

'What year?'

'1820s, I think,' replied Jake. 'You'll be lucky to find another one of this quality.'

'It's beautiful. Where did it come from?'

'Come on, Sash, you know better than to ask that, but I can tell you it's not local.'

'Okay, now the big question: how much?'

'Well, if it was legit, you'd be looking at five-hundred quid, but I can let you have it for, what shall we say, two-fifty. How does that sound?'

'Would you take two-hundred?'

'Nah, you know what it's worth, and I know what I can get for it.'

'Okay then, I'll just get your money.'

She looked furtive and guilty as she turned and saw Lenny looking at her with a big grin on his face. He was enjoying every minute of it. How the hell am I going to explain this away? she thought.

'Look, I can explain…'

'There's no explanation needed,' said Lenny, revelling in what he had just witnessed.

Sasha took the money from a drawer in the escritoire and handed it to Jake.

'Thank you.'

'My pleasure,' said Jake. 'See you next time.' And, with a quick look at Lenny, he was gone.

'So that's how you do it,' said Lenny.

'Do what?'

'Afford to buy antiques. It's your little secret; your way around the problem of being able to buy the more expensive items.'

There was little point in trying to deny it; I may as well come clean, she thought. 'Yes, okay, I admit I buy knock-off antiques.'

'May I?' he said, holding out his hand. Sasha passed him the candlestick holder. 'It's certainly a lovely piece, and very desirable too.'

'While you're drooling over it, can I get you another drink?' said Sasha, picking up his glass.

'Do you really have to ask?'

'I suppose it was a daft question.'

Sasha replenished his glass once more, and when she sat down, she said, 'Look, you will keep it to yourself, won't you? I don't want it to be common knowledge that I buy stolen antiques.'

'Of course, I won't breathe a word. Your secret is safe with me.'

'How do I know I can trust you?'

'I don't suppose you do, but maybe…'

'Maybe what?'

'Well, I don't know.'

'What don't you know?'

'It's just possible we may be able to help one another.'

'How? What are you trying to say?' said an exasperated Sasha.

'Well, I mentioned earlier how I supplemented my income by doing a bit of wheeling and dealing.'

'Yes. Is this going to be the big reveal – your secret?'

'Er, I suppose it is, yes.'

'Don't forget your drink,' she said eagerly.

'As if,' said Lenny, picking up his glass. 'I could do for you what your friend Jake does.'

'Really? How so?'

'Well, shall we say, from time to time, things come into my possession and I need an outlet for them.'

'What are you saying, that you're a middleman? That's only going to bump up the price.'

'Er, no. I'm not a middleman. I can supply you direct.'

'Ah, that's different,' said Sasha. 'Where do you get the stuff from?'

'Here and there. I travel a bit in my job, I go to various hotels and apartment buildings, etcetera, and the beauty of it is, nobody takes any notice of a lift engineer.'

'I guess that's where the other meaning of "Lenny the Lift" comes from.'

'Correct.'

'Well, I noticed, so don't go getting any ideas about turning over this place.'

'I wouldn't; you'd be a customer. But I don't just rely on those types of buildings, they are more opportunistic, if you know what I mean. God, I can't believe I'm having this conversation.'

'Oh, you are, believe me, do carry on.'

'Look, I guess this puts us on an equal footing, doesn't it? We know where we stand; we can't afford to drop each other in it.'

'No, and it makes me breathe a bit easier knowing that,' said Sasha. 'But you were saying… about other jobs?'

'Oh, yeah. I do occasionally break into larger houses:

there are richer pickings to be had. But I've learnt to go for smaller items as they are easier to move on. You can end up being stuck with larger items.'

'Have you ever been caught?'

'No, but I've had one or two close shaves,' said Lenny, warming to his confessional.

'Go on then, tell me.'

'There was one occasion, about three years ago, and it concerns a piece of silver I couldn't get rid of, in fact, I've still got the damn thing. Actually, it might be of interest to you, now I think about it.'

'Really? What is it?'

'It's a silver claret jug circa 1860s, it's a beautiful, distinctive piece, which is why I haven't been able to shift it. I did some research and apparently it is known as the Railway Presentation Armada Claret Jug, made by Stephen and William Nicholson. It's worth about five grand, but, of course, we can do a deal.'

Sasha sat there rather pensive, her mind seemingly elsewhere. Her thought process was working in slow motion, it was like wading through a salt marsh. Her mind desperately trying to play catch up. Bells were ringing.

'Well?'

'Well, what?' said Sasha, being pulled back into the here and now.

'Would you be interested in having a look at it?'

'I don't suppose it would do any harm.'

'Okay, I'll bring it over and you can see what you think. Anyway, as I was saying, I broke into this country house one night, just outside Cambridge.'

'Whereabouts?'

'Does it matter?'

'Well, yes, I'd like to know.'

'I think – if I remember correctly – it was just on the edge of a little village off the Newmarket Road out of Cambridge.'

'Really? I don't suppose you can remember the name of the village, can you? said Sasha, hanging on to every word.

'No, I can't. Why are you so interested? Are you okay? You look as if something is troubling you.'

'No, no. Sorry, it's just…I'm all right. Please carry on.'

'Okay. Well, I got into the house in the small hours and it was all quiet. There was quite a bit of gear to be had, so I was filling my bag as quickly and quietly as I could, when suddenly the lights came on. There stood this old biddy demanding to know what I was doing; I mean, how stupid can you get? I tried to get past her, but she grabbed hold of me and I had to wrestle myself free, and, in the process, I pushed her backwards and she went down, banging her head on the corner of the hearth.'

Sasha stared at Lenny, her mouth gaping, as the gradual realization of what he had done dawned on her. She bit her bottom lip as she tried to stay composed.

'She laid there motionless: I panicked. I had to get away. I wasn't going to hang around, so I picked up my bag and made a run for it. And that's where I got the claret jug from. I later found out the old woman had died.'

'Y—You killed her.' was all that Sasha could say.

'It wasn't intentional. You sure you're alright?'

Sasha's head was swimming. She knew she had to do something but not what it should be. She now felt wide awake, and the reality made her fearful of what might happen. 'Y—Yes, I'm—I'm okay. I—um—I'm feeling a bit peckish. I'll just go and get us some nibbles, help yourself to another drink.'

Sasha made slow, deliberate moves as she got up out of her chair, and tried not to run to the kitchen. She didn't want to arouse any suspicion that the situation was anything other than normal.

Once in the kitchen, Sasha closed the door behind her and took out her phone and dialed.

'Hello, emergency, which service do you require?'

'Police, please.'

'Police, what's the nature of the emergency?'

'There's a murderer in my apartment. It's on the top floor—'

Suddenly, the door burst open and there stood Lenny brandishing the wooden club. He was angry. Gone was the smiling, affable bloke she had been drinking with and exchanging secrets.

'You shouldn't have done that, you really shouldn't,' he said, advancing menacingly towards her.

'Number thirty-seven, Fern House, Crossley Road. Please hurry he's—'

Lenny snatched away her phone and threw it on the floor, then stamped on it with his size ten. 'Why did you have to do that?' he snarled. 'I thought we had an understanding.'

'The woman—the woman you murdered was—was my mother.'

'Your mother?'

'Yes, and you'll pay for that; the police are on the way.'

Lenny glared at her with hatred in his eyes, his face black as thunder. 'I can't let you tell the police what happened; you have to be silenced.'

'They'll be here in a few minutes. You'll—You'll never get away with it.' shrieked Sasha, backing away. She came up against a cupboard and instinctively grabbed a knife from the worktop.

'You, stupid bitch,' said Lenny, as he raised the club.

She lunged wildly at him with the knife, missed and lost her balance. 'No! No! Please!' screamed Sasha, as she cowered before him. But it was too late.

There was a sickening crunch as the club came crashing down on her head. Lenny continued to rain down blows with a pathological frenzy until his anger was spent. He stood, breathing heavily, looking at the bloodied, lifeless body, not quite believing what he had done. Why, oh, why did she have to do that?

But now he had to get away, and fast, before the police arrived. He ran out of the apartment and down the corridor, stopping at the junction of the lift and the stairs. Lenny plumped for the lift, as it would be quicker. He pressed the call button, willing the lift to be empty.

He got his wish.

He hurried into the lift and pressed G. As the lift descended, Lenny leaned backwards on the wall, closed his eyes and breathed a sigh of relief.

Suddenly, there was a loud clunk and the lift shuddered to a halt between levels four and five.

The lift had broken down yet again.

On a Cold Winter's Night

'And where do you think you're going?'

'Out,' said Roger emphatically, trying to stamp his authority.

'Well, you hadn't better be getting up to any of your old tricks, or else,' said Jenny, his wife.

'W—What do you mean?' he said, suddenly taken aback.

'You know very well what I mean. You're not the only one at it.'

'What? You're not…'

'I'm not anything.'

'But…'

'Roger, you're looking guilty.'

'Who? Me?'

'You're the only other person in this room, so I guess it must be you I'm talking to.'

'I've got nothing to feel guilty about. What are you

insinuating?' he said tremulously.

'Relax,' said Jenny, with the hint of a smile. 'Where are you going?'

'You know where – to the bridge club.'

'And what do you do when you're playing?'

'Try to win…ah, I get it, tricks. Up to my old tricks. For a moment, there, I thought you were talking about something else.'

'Is that why you looked so guilty? Is there something I should know about? Did you want to tell me anything?'

'Er, no. No, of course not. If there was anything going on, I'm sure Freya, your ears and eyes, would have told you. There's nothing going on in the bridge club that she doesn't know about.'

'And just you remember that,' said Jenny, not entirely convinced by his rebuttal. But he was right, she thought, Freya would tell her if anything was going on. They didn't keep secrets from each other; they were bosom buddies. 'I didn't think you would be going, anyway. Haven't you got a deadline to meet?'

'Yes, I have, but I need a break from it for a few hours to refresh my mind – it works wonders. My publisher will still get the manuscript on time. Right, must go. See you later. Unfortunately,' he added under his breath, as he went out the door.

The rawness of the cutting wind, howling down from the

north that December evening, took Roger's breath away as he walked from his car to the village hall. On entering, he was met by a wall of heat. It was like standing in front of a furnace. It felt so good as the warmth went to work on his extremities. There was a good turn-out for such a bitter evening, but, then, it was their last meeting before Christmas and there would be festive nibbles and wine.

Roger hung his coat up and walked into the room, only to find Freya, who was wearing a Christmas jumper, making a beeline for him. Her dark hair was shiny and luxuriant. Her brown eyes sparkling beneath a fringe.

'Hello, Roger, I'm so pleased you were able to make it. It means we can pair up as usual.'

'Oh, good. I do like pairing up with you.'

'Play your cards right and we can pair up afterwards, as well,' she said, with a twinkle in her eye.

'That's what I meant. Why do you think I come to these bridge evenings, if it's not to pair up with you?'

'I know I can always depend on you to come up trumps.'

'But only when it suits, and you lay your cards on the table,' said Roger.

'Okay, I give up. You win in spades full. I can't come up with anymore puns.'

'I guess you just haven't got the heart for it.'

'Aaaargh. Stop it! Or I'll club you!'

'What are you two laughing about?' said Gideon, the

club secretary, as he came up to them.

'We were just having a bit of fun with a play on words,' said Roger.

'Oh, I see, jolly good. You two are down to play Jon and Claire for the first rubber,' he said, looking at his clipboard. 'There will be food and wine when we've finished this evening. I do hope you'll be able to stay for a bit of a get-together.'

We'll be having our own get-together, thought Freya. Don't you worry about that.

The evening passed very pleasantly with Roger and Freya coming out on top. They felt obliged to stay for a little while afterwards, though they were both eager to get away.

'Look, we can't be seen to leave at the same time,' said Freya. 'I'll go first and you slip away as soon as you can, and I'll see you back at mine.'

'Yeah, okay,' said Roger, before moving away to mix with the other members.

Roger pulled up outside Freya's house, full of eager anticipation. It was only times spent with her that kept him going. Life at home was somewhat dull and dreary. The love between him and Jenny had long-since evaporated, but they rubbed along in a perfunctory manner. He kept writing the books: she kept spending the royalties. But Freya had given him a glimpse of what life could be like – and he liked what he saw.

Roger turned his collar against the wind and knocked on the door.

'Come in, quick before the cold gets in,' said Freya, opening the door.

Safely ensconced, Roger removed his coat.

'Well, don't stop there,' she said, moving to help him out of his trousers.

'You don't hang about, do you? What's the rush? Are you on the clock?'

'I've been waiting for this moment. All evening, I've been sitting opposite you full of yearning. A woman has certain needs, you know.'

'Steady on, love. Can we not, at least, go to bed?'

'No. Where's your spontaneity? Your gay abandon? Roger, I need you to take me now!'

They quickly divested each other of clothes and kissed with an urgency Roger had never known. They lowered themselves onto a rug, with racing pulses and thumping hearts. Freya hungered for him with the very essence of her being. She was ravenous – wild with desire.

Roger's tongue delicately traced a line from her breasts, down her stomach to her mons verenis. Freya arched her back, thrusting herself forward, eager for him to explore her.

She turned him onto his back and started kissing him

all over. Freya went down to his feet, gently and rhythmically sucking his big toe, which sent waves of ecstasy radiating through his body. A sensation he had never experienced before. They could not contain themselves any longer so Freya straddled him as they worked themselves into a rapturous climax.

As they laid there, post coital, Freya said, 'I wish you didn't have to go. I can't carry on like this for much longer, it's tearing me apart.'

'I know. It won't always be like this, and I do really want to be with you. If I leave her, she'll take me for every penny I've got, and I want us to have a comfortable life together.'

'So, what's the answer? Seemingly, it will always be the case.'

'I don't know,' admitted Roger.

'There is a way.'

'Really? How?'

'You could always do away with her.'

'What? You can't be serious.'

'Why not?'

'Why not? Because I would end up in prison for the rest of my natural, that's why not. And we wouldn't be together, which would defeat the whole objective of the exercise.'

'But only if you get caught.'

'How on earth do you think I could murder Jenny and

get away with it? It's just not possible.'

'Anything is possible. I'm sure Roger Brooke, author of bestselling thrillers, can come up with a method which is foolproof,' said Freya.

'You're crazy,' he said. 'I write fiction, where anything can happen. This is real life, where those things just do not happen.'

'Oh, come on. With a brain like yours, I'm sure you can come up with something. You do it in your novels. You just need to get those little grey cells working. I'm sure you could arrange for an *'accident'* to happen.'

'Can you hear yourself? You're saying I should murder my wife. Do you realise the enormity of what you're saying? You actually want me to kill another human being in cold blood.'

'Is the prize not worth it? Do you really want to be with me?'

It was at that point, Roger thought, oh my god, she's deadly serious.

* * *

'What time did you get in last night? It was late,' said Jenny.

'Yeah, I know. We had a bit of a soiree after we finished, as it was the last meeting before Christmas,' explained Roger.

'So, what did you get up to?'

'What do you mean?'

'Exactly what I said. What did you get up to?'

'Oh, you mean Freya hasn't rung to tell you all the sordid details? Heavens above. Well, we all got together in a circle and threw our car keys into the middle.'

'Very funny.'

'No, it wasn't – I came away with a Reliant Robin,' he quipped.

'What's put you in a good mood?'

'Oh, you know. The joy of life. Being married to you. Christmas is coming. Probably all three.'

'You're up to something.'

'Really? You think so? Like what?'

'I don't know but I'll find out,' she said.

* * *

'No, it was a nice evening, really,' said Freya. 'Roger and I won our rubbers and then we had a bit of a get together afterwards with some petits fours and wine. Where is Roger, anyway?'

'Oh, he's in his writing room as usual; he has a deadline to meet,' said Jenny. 'Tell me, did you notice anything different about him the other night?'

'What do you mean? Like what?'

'Well, since that night, he's been in a good mood, which is unusual for him and unsettling for me. I just wondered if something had happened to cause this change.'

'Er, no. I think he just enjoyed the evening's events,' said Freya with a smile.

'Must have done, I suppose. How are you? I imagine you must find it a bit difficult at this time of the year, since your divorce.'

'Well, yes, I won't lie to you, it does reinforce the loneliness. But I've got no regrets about getting rid of that lying, cheating scumbag. And I shall forever be indebted to you for all the help and support you gave me – you both gave me – to see me through that nightmare. I wouldn't have got through it without you.'

'So, have you not met anyone else over these past three years?'

'No, not really. To be honest, I'm a bit wary of getting bitten again. I need to learn how to build up trust, it's not easy.'

'It must be difficult, I suppose, but you're still young enough to start again,' said Jenny.

'Huh, you call forty-five young?'

'Yes, and you're very attractive to go with it. You'll meet someone.'

'When you're my age, all the good ones are spoken for,' said Freya. 'I don't suppose you've ever thought what you'd do if Roger was carrying on behind your back?'

'I'd make sure that both of them regretted it. You've

got no idea what lengths I'd go to.'

'So, you wouldn't just divorce him and move on, glad to see the back of him?'

'Oh, no. I would never make things easy for him by giving him what he wants. He would pay dearly for his liaison.'

'Sounds like you'd be a formidable adversary.'

'You'd better believe it, or, rather, he should,' said Jenny. 'Can I get you another cup of tea?'

'Thank you. Yes, I'd love one.'

As Jenny went to the kitchen, Freya got up and went to look at her collection of Swarovski cut glass crystal figurines which were housed in a display cabinet. There was a magnificent pair of bald eagles doing battle with their talons. The piece was absolutely stunning. Freya couldn't even begin to imagine what it must be worth. It probably ran into thousands.

'Here we go, fresh tea and a mince pie, seeing as it's nearly Christmas. Is Imogen coming to yours for Christmas this year?' said Jenny.

'Sadly, not. She's going straight from uni to her father's, in Windermere. But she is coming to spend the new year with me.'

'Right, you must come to us for Christmas. We can't have you spending it on your own.'

'No, I couldn't possibly…'

'Nonsense, my woman, you're coming and that's it.'

'But what about Roger?' said Freya.

'What about him?'

'He might not want me here.'

'Don't be so daft, he'd love to have you. So, it's all settled then – you're coming to us. I don't want to hear another word.'

'Well, thank you, you're most kind. I'm looking forward to it already.'

* * *

It was two days later, as Jenny was decorating the Christmas tree, that the phone rang. She picked it up to find it was Freya.

'I'm sorry to trouble you,' said Freya. 'And I wouldn't have done so if it wasn't necessary.'

'It's perfectly alright. How can I help?'

'Well, you can't because you don't drive. The thing is, my car won't start and I have a dental appointment at eleven. If I don't turn up, they will charge me. So, I wondered if Roger would be a dear and take me. I know he's busy but do you think he could find the time to give me a lift?'

'I'm sure he would: I'll send him straight away.'

'Oh, thank you. You've saved the day.'

Roger pulled up outside Freya's house, and she came running down the path and climbed into the car. 'Thanks for rescuing me. That bloody car just wouldn't start.'

'Oh, it's genuine, is it?' said a disappointed Roger.

'Of course, it is, why else would I have called you out?'

'Well, I didn't know if it was for *"personal services"*. You could have been in need of squiring for all I knew.'

'I'm always in need of that,' she said, 'but right now I need to be at the dentist's.'

Roger let the clutch up and floored the accelerator. They took off like a drag car at Santa Pod Raceway, the force throwing them back into the seats.

'We'll have you there in no time.'

'I would rather *there* be the dentist than the mortuary,' said Freya, alarmed by the speed they were doing.

'There's no need to worry, you're in safe hands.'

'How do you feel about me coming to yours for Christmas? Only, Jenny was most insistent about it.'

'I think it will be great; I'm really looking forward to it,' said Roger.

'Really?'

'Yes. It will be enjoyable. Usually, it's pretty dreary with only the two of us and there's never much bonhomie.'

'You won't find it a bit, er, awkward?'

'No, but it could be a bit frustrating, though, you being so close and, yet, untouchable.'

'Have you had any more thoughts about what we

discussed the other evening?' said Freya.

'What, you mean bumping her off?'

'Yes, that's exactly what I mean. I've already told you, I can't carry on like this. You've got to do something. Jenny made it abundantly clear, the other day, what she would do if she found out you were having an affair. There would be no amicable divorce and living happily ever after. She would make both our lives hell. So, there is no other option, you've got to come up with a plan. If you don't, there cannot be a future for us.'

'How on earth do you think I'm going to do that and get away with it? I wouldn't, and that, too, would mean no future for us. What am I supposed to do?'

'As a writer, you have a very fertile and imaginative mind – use it.'

Roger was exasperated. He was in a desperate situation. He wanted to be with her more than anything, yet she was giving him an impossible ultimatum. Murdering someone in a story was one thing, but to do it in real life was something else. Was there a way of doing it and getting away with it? He doubted it.

'Look, it's not easy to come up with a plan, in fact, it's downright difficult. Have you got any bright ideas?'

'No. I'm not the expert. That's your department, but you need to do something - and soon.'

'Okay, okay, I'll give it some serious thought. But it will take time if it's to be foolproof.'

'I have every confidence in you,' she said.

It was a ponderous Roger who returned home an hour later, weighed down by the thought of what was expected of him. Sitting at his desk, he was unable to focus his mind on the novel he was writing. He didn't respond well to pressure, but now he was faced with a double dose: to get the book finished, and to come up with a plan to do away with his wife.

Sleep would not come easy that night.

* * *

Christmas day dawned cold and frosty. The temperature had barely climbed above freezing for the past few days. Roger looked out of the window and surveyed the wintry scene before him. The frost on the rails of the garden fence was glistening in the weak, milky sun of the early morning. However, there were ominous clouds forming in the distance. Maybe snow for later, he mused. But there was also a cloud still hanging over him, which showed no signs of abating. Today is Christmas, he thought, and Freya is coming. Maybe he could put all those thoughts and worries to one side for the day and try to enjoy it.

Wife permitting.

Freya arrived at midday, bearing gifts and a bottle of

Prosecco. 'Happy Christmas!' she said, kissing them both.

'Yes, happy Christmas.'

'Happy Christmas,' echoed Roger.

'It's lovely to see you. I'm so glad you were able to come,' said Jenny.

'I'm pleased to be here. Thank you for inviting me.'

'How are the roads?' said Roger. 'Is it still freezing?'

'Yes, it is. The main roads are okay, they've been gritted, but these back roads are a bit treacherous. And there were a few flakes of snow, as well.'

'Yes, I think we're due to get some snow, so we might have a white Christmas, which would be unusual,' said Roger.

'Right, I've got everything under control,' said Jenny. 'The turkey is nearly done and the vegetables are all prepared and ready. Would you like a glass of wine? I've got a bottle already opened. I'll put yours in the fridge.'

'Thank you, I'd love one.'

'Help yourself if you want one, Roger.'

'Charming,' he said, rolling his eyes.'

'Let's take our drinks through to the living room and open our gifts,' said Jenny.

'Oh, look, it's starting to snow!' exclaimed Freya.

'It's bound to settle as the ground is frozen,' said Roger. 'Still, it's very scenic, isn't it?'

After exchanging and opening gifts, Jenny got up and

said, 'I'm just going to check on the turkey and put the vegetables on. Back in a mo.'

'It's so nice to be spending Christmas with you,' said Freya. 'If things were different, we could have spent the night together, as well. Wouldn't that have been nice?'

'Yes, if only.'

'Well, what are you going to do about it?'

'Please, not now. Not today.'

'Have you had any ideas? Made any plans? I want to be with you, Roger. Don't you want to be with me?

'Yes, of course I do. You know I do.'

'Well, then?'

'I'm working on it. It's not easy: it takes time.'

'Time is slipping by, lover boy. You need to be more proactive.'

'Right, I've taken the turkey out and left it to stand, and I've put the veggies on. Should be ready in about fifteen to twenty minutes,' said Jenny, as she entered the room. What were you two talking about?'

'We were just talking about ideas and plans for Roger's next book,' said Freya. 'About a man who plans to murder his wife so he can be with his lover.'

Roger's eyes nearly popped out of their sockets. He looked daggers at Freya. What the hell was she playing at?'

'It's…er, only an idea at the moment,' he said, somewhat shaken.

'Yes, it just needs firming up,' said Freya, looking him in the eye.

'Maybe you two should collaborate,' said Jenny.

'Oh, no,' replied Freya. 'Roger is the expert, I'll leave it to him.'

'Are you all right, Roger? You look unsettled. Is something troubling you?'

'I, er. I need to, I've just got to…' he mumbled, as he quickly got up and left the room.

'Was it something I said?' asked Jenny. 'How strange.'

'Maybe he's just had an idea and has gone to jot it down before he forgets. You know what these writers are like.'

'I'm well and truly stuffed,' said Roger, as he placed his knife and fork on the empty plate.

'Yes, me too. That was lovely. Thank you,' said Freya. 'I don't think I can move.'

'I hope you've left room for Christmas pud,' said Jenny.

'Oh, no!'

'I couldn't possibly.'

'Okay, maybe later, then.'

'How about we go sit down and let it digest for a bit and then Roger and I will do the washing up?'

'Sounds like a plan,' said Jenny.

'You know, the snow is still coming down quite hard. There's about six inches, or more, in places. If it carries on like this, we'll be snowed in,' said Roger.

'Anybody up for playing a game of something, or other?' said Jenny.

'What have you got?' asked Freya.

'Well, there's Monopoly, of course. Cards, Trivial Pursuit…'

'Have you got Cluedo?'

'No, sorry, we haven't got that.'

'That's a pity. It might have given Roger a few ideas about who did what to whom, with which weapon and in which room.' Freya gave Roger a saccharin smile as she said it.

Has she taken leave of her senses? thought Roger. For Christ sake, she could put the whole idea in jeopardy if she's not careful. She needs to watch her tongue.

'Why would Roger want ideas about murdering people?'

'For his books, of course,' said Freya. 'It must be difficult trying to come up with new ideas.'

'Oh, I see what you mean. For a moment, I thought you meant he was planning to actually kill someone.'

'No, I don't think he's got the bottle to do that,' said Freya, giving him a meaningful look.

'I should think not,' said Jenny.

Roger squirmed uncomfortably in his chair.

'Anybody fancy something to eat? I've got loads,' said Jenny.

'No, not really. I'm still feeling full from lunch,' said Freya.

'I could do with a sandwich, or something. What about you?' she said, looking at Roger.

'I suppose I could force something down,' he replied.

'Okay, I'll just make a plate of sandwiches and a few nibbles to bring through here, then you can help yourselves,' she said, getting up and going to the kitchen.

'Just what do you think you're playing at?' blazed Roger.

'I don't know what you mean.'

'Don't play the innocent with me. You know exactly what I mean. All those references to me…to me kil— you know what.'

'But I thought you were up for it. I thought you wanted to be with me,' said Freya. 'I can't carry on like this for much longer. You've got to do something, my darling.'

'Yes, okay, I will. But you applying pressure, is making it harder for me to think. You're putting me on edge. I don't know what you're going to come out with next. And if Jenny twigs what's going on, it will never happen. So, back off.'

'Yes, okay, Roger. I'm sorry, but you have to understand how much I love you and want to be with you.

It's torture having to share you.'

'Look, I'm on it, okay?'

'I don't think you're going to be able to get home tonight, Freya,' said Jenny, placing a tray on the coffee table. 'The snow is deeper than ever and it's still coming down.'

'Oh, dear, I didn't realise.'

'It's okay, you can stay the night; it's not a problem.'

'Are you sure?'

'Of course, I'm sure. These back roads will be impassable.'

'Are you sure you're alright, Freya? You don't look too good,' said Jenny.

'To be honest, I don't feel very well. I don't know what it is. Maybe I've eaten too much.'

'Well, you haven't had anything we haven't had, and we're both all right,' said Roger.

'I don't feel very warm, either,' said Freya.

'Do you think you may be coming down with flu?' said Jenny.

'Possibly. I don't really know. I'm sure it will pass, it's nothing to worry about.'

'I know what you need,' said Roger, getting up. 'A hot toddy. It never fails; I'll go and get you one.'

'Would you like me to get you a sweater to put on and warm yourself up a bit?' said Jenny.

'No, it's okay, I'm fine. I'm sure I'll warm up in a bit when I've had that hot toddy.'

'I'm not sure it's the right kind of medication to have.'

'Well, it's worth trying. There's a lot to be said for these old remedies that have been passed down through the generations,' said Freya with a wan smile.

'Shall we see what's on the television?'

'It will only be the usual crap,' said Freya. Though you might find something on BBC2 or BBC4.'

'Well, let's have a look,' she said, picking up the television guide. 'The Sleeping Beauty is on BBC4, if you enjoy ballet.'

'Oh, yes, I do.'

'Okay, we'll watch it, then.'

'Oh, no. It's got to be something we all want to watch. You mustn't put it on just to please me,' said Freya.

'I would like to watch it.'

'Really?'

'Yes, really.'

'What about Roger?'

'Don't worry about him. If he doesn't like it – tough.'

'That's hardly fair.'

'Of course, it is. We're in the majority,' said Jenny, reaching for the remote.

'Here we are, one prescription dispensed. The dose should be repeated at regular intervals until the symptoms subside,' said Roger, handing Freya the hot toddy.

'Thank you, doctor. I feel sure if I had enough of them, they would cure anything – eventually,' she said.

'What are we watching, then?'

'We are going to watch a ballet,' said Jenny.

'A ballet?'

'Yep, a ballet.'

'Oh, okay. I'm always willing to try something different.'

'Well, much to my surprise, I quite enjoyed that,' said Roger. 'It was all very artistic and graceful.'

'I do believe we have a convert,' said Jenny. 'Freya, are you alright? You're shivering.'

'Yes, I don't feel well at all.'

'Come on, let's get you to bed, and I'll get you a couple of Paracetamol.'

'I'm so sorry,' said Freya.

'Nonsense, my girl. You've got nothing to be sorry about. If you can get a good night's sleep, you'll feel so much better in the morning.'

'Yes, I'm sure I will. Good night, Roger, and thanks for the hot toddy, even though it didn't work.'

'It's a bit like antibiotics: you have to take the full course for it to be effective. Anyway, you try and get a good night's sleep and I'll see you in the morning.'

'You can get me a large Baileys; I'll be down in a minute,' said Jenny.

'Yes, Herr Commandant,' replied Roger, getting to his feet and clicking his heels. He was sick and tired of the way she treated him, he never got a *"please"* or a *"thank you"*. For too long he had put up with it just to have a quieter life, but a man can only take so much.

Roger poured her a glass of Baileys, and himself a large single malt, then sat down again and turned his mind to ways of doing away with his wife. Was there such a thing as the perfect murder? he wondered; one that was undetectable? Probably not. So, what on earth was he going to do? He was committed to being with Freya, but how was he going to engineer that happening?

'What are you so deep in thought about?' said Jenny, sitting down and picking up her drink.

'You really wouldn't want to know.'

'Try me.'

'My god, are you actually trying to have a conversation with me?'

'Why is that concept so difficult for you to comprehend?'

'Oh, I don't really know, now let me think. Could it be the way you constantly bark out orders without so much as a *"please"* or *"thank you"*? Or could it be because you never take an interest in anything I do? Could it be the way you sit in front of the television night after night, ignoring me? Could it be because you never ask my opinion on anything? Take your pick. It's always your way or the highway.'

'Whatever's got into you? Where did all that come from?'

'The fact, you've had to ask, is proof of what I said. You never pay any attention to me. All I am to you is a meal ticket.'

'That is not true,' she said.

'Really? We never do anything together. We lead separate lives. This marriage was over years ago.'

'If that's the case, why haven't you left me?'

'Because you would bleed me dry.'

'I would do more than that.'

'You see, I'm right. You've just confirmed it. You are a nasty, vindictive, money-grabbing, self-centred cow.'

'I'm not listening to this. I've had enough gassing to you. I'm going to bed and you can go to hell.' With that, Jenny stormed out of the room and up the stairs.

Roger sat there, his mind ticking over, when he had a lightbulb moment. Gassing, she'd said, but of course, that was it. It was the perfect, foolproof way of killing her. A wave of joyous relief washed over him as he relaxed with his whisky and bided his time. It was going to happen: he and Freya could be together after all.

And it was so simple.

Two hours later, Roger got up from his chair and went to the gas meter, confident that his wife would now be asleep. She always kept the gas fire on in their bedroom through the night when it was cold. He pulled the lever down to turn the off the gas and waited. After a few minutes, when he was sure the remaining gas in the pipe had been used up and the flame extinguished, he turned the gas back on. The bedroom would now fill with gas through the night and, subsequently, kill his wife whilst she slept.

His work done, Roger went to the spare bedroom at the front of the house to sleep, safe in the knowledge he would be a free man come the morning.

* * *

The following morning, Roger came down the stairs in a buoyant mood. This was the first day of the rest of his life. He cheerfully made himself breakfast and allowed himself to look ahead at what the future might hold.

As he was drinking his coffee, he heard footsteps coming down the stairs. 'In here darling,' he called out. 'Great news; I've done it. We're free.'

'And what exactly have you done *darling?*'

Roger turned to see the imposing figure of his wife standing in the doorway. 'W—What…er, I,' he was floundering. Lost for words. Shocked to see her standing there.

'What's the matter with you? You look like you've

seen a ghost. You weren't so short of words last night.'

'But...But...you...should—'

'I should what?'

'How's—How's Freya this morning?'

'I don't know, I've not checked on her. I put her in our room last night as it had the heater in there to keep her warm.'

'Whaaa...'

Still Waters

Evelyn sat in a chair, head bowed, not saying anything as her husband, Horry, paced back and forth, his anger simmering away. Any minute now, she knew she would be on the receiving end of yet another tirade of abuse. For more years than she cared to remember, Evelyn had been subjected to his bullying and belittling. She had long since given up trying to defend herself. How could she stand up to this brute of a man who was physically and mentally stronger than her? She was no match for him in any department, so she suffered in silence. The ticking of the grandfather clock was counting down the seconds to the inevitable onslaught. The anticipation was playing havoc with her nerves. Why didn't he just get on with it?

Suddenly, he was there, towering above her.

'Can you not get anything right, you useless apology for a woman? You're incapable of following the simplest of instructions. I asked you to do one thing for me – just one – and you managed to balls it up. Where were you when they were handing out brains? You stupid cretin.'

Evelyn continued to look down, silently staring at the threadbare carpet, her leg involuntarily twitching. It was best to let him rant and rave, get it out of his system. There was no other way to deal with his irrationality.

'You had two things to do when you went into town: pick up your prescription and get me a can of oil. Miraculously, you remembered your pills, but when you went to the hardware store, what did you do? You brought back a tin of grease. Do you not know the difference? you imbecile.'

There was no way Evelyn would have forgotten her pills. They were the only things which kept her going. Her depression was the direct result of her husband's treatment of her. Years of absorbing the constant beration had taken their toll. Leaving wasn't an option because she had nowhere to go and she was frightened of what her husband's reaction would be. He would never let her leave, so she remained trapped in this abusive, loveless marriage.

'Why the hell I agreed to marry you, I'll never know,' he continued. 'You're no use to man nor beast – a complete waste of space. I should have you put down but, then, I'm not given to acts of kindness.'

Evelyn thought it might be a good idea. It was

seemingly the only way she could think of to get out of this miserable existence which passed as life. Many was the time she had considered taking all of her pills in one go, but what if it didn't work and she was left with damaged organs? It would make life even worse than it was now, if that were possible.

'What have you got to say for yourself? Look at me when I'm talking to you.'

Evelyn slowly raised her head to find him standing there, fists clenched.

'Well?' he growled.

She shook her head as a solitary tear escaped the watery reservoir of her eye, and her head dropped again. She couldn't look at him. She wanted the floor to open up and swallow her. Evelyn would rather be anywhere but here. How had it come to this? After nearly fifty years of marriage, she was living in fear of her husband. If she were to say something, it would only add fuel to her husband's ire, and there was no telling what he might do.

'You're pathetic, do you know that? What goes on in that silent little world you inhabit?'

Evelyn couldn't understand why he was like this, there was no need for it. Horry had become more cantankerous the older he got. Everything that went wrong was her fault. If it was raining, it was her fault. No matter what, it was always her fault. Why? Why did he do it?

'Why is it, everything you do you get it wrong? You

couldn't even get it right when you were carrying our baby, could you?

Evelyn sobbed. She knew it wouldn't be long before he dragged that up again. How could he be so cruel? She had never been able to come to terms with losing her baby. There was no bereavement counselling in those days. Her husband didn't speak to her for two weeks after that, and she was left to deal with the aftermath of that devastating experience on her own.

'Ha, touched a nerve, did I? Had you forgotten about your ignominious attempt to become a mother? Something other women manage without too much trouble. But you, you managed to make it all end in tears, and, to cap it all, there was no chance of being able to try again.'

Evelyn's shoulders pumped up and down in a rhythmic fashion as the raw emotion flowed freely. He really knew how to stick the knife in and then give it a twist. The pain pulsated like the relentless beat of a throbbing bass drum. It became too much for her: she had to escape. In a blind panic, she quickly jumped up, causing a surprised Horry to take a step backwards, and fled the room. Her body's response to a sensory overload. It was, very much, fight or flight.

'That's right. Run away when the going gets tough and the truth comes out,' Horry called after her, as she ran up the stairs.

She flung herself onto the bed and sobbed and sobbed until eventually she drifted into a peaceful and restorative slumber.

It was some two hours later when Evelyn woke up and, for a few moments, she wondered how she came to be lying on the bed fully clothed. Then gradually the mist began to clear and it all came back to her. All the horrible, nasty, hurtful things that had been hurled at her. How could one human being be so spiteful towards another? If there was any justice in this world, surely, he would get his comeuppance?

Evelyn went down the stairs, unsure of what her reception would be. It wouldn't be welcoming, that's for sure. The best she could hope for was silence. Silence is Golden – a song she remembered from her youth. Those happy, heady days when life was good and full of adventure. How had it all come to this?

Gingerly, she cracked open the living room door, her heart in her mouth. She paused briefly, waiting for a reaction. There wasn't any. So, she opened the door wider and walked in to find Horry with his head in a newspaper.

'I'll have a cuppa if you're making one,' he said, without looking up.

It wasn't a request it was a demand. Evelyn knew that, so she turned and went into the kitchen. She didn't mind, as she intended to make herself one, anyway. When she returned, carrying the cups on a tray, Horry was fiddling with the television. Evelyn placed the tray on the coffee table and sat down in a chair without saying a word. So far, so good, she thought. He hadn't mentioned what happened earlier.

'Bloody television. It's playing up again. I can't get a picture. It had to happen tonight when the football was on, didn't it? Why couldn't it happen when your Coronation Street is on? A night when it didn't matter. The aerial probably needs adjusting. Well, I'm not paying someone to do a job I can do myself. It will have to wait until tomorrow now; it's dark.'

Evelyn was concerned about the television not working because it meant her husband would not be engrossed watching it. That meant there was a greater risk of him turning his attention to her.

'I'll need you to help me with the aerial,' said Horry. 'You'll need to be in here with the television on and the window open. As I turn the aerial, you'll have to shout when there's a picture. Even you shouldn't be able to mess that up, though I wouldn't be taking any bets on that. Did you understand what I just said, you bird-brained dimwit?'

Evelyn gave a reticent, half-hearted nod of her head. She was dreading it. She knew that if things didn't go well, she would be on the receiving end of yet another outburst of anger and vilification.

Sleep wouldn't come easily that night.

* * *

The following morning, Evelyn was up bright and early as usual. She liked to get up before her husband so she could have a relaxed breakfast in peace and quiet. It also allowed her time to get a few things done without the constant surveillance. She would make sure to check there wasn't anything out of place or needing doing before her husband came down and started finding fault.

It was a way of life Evelyn had grown accustomed to, and, over the years, she had withdrawn more and more into her shell. The happy-go-lucky girl of yesteryear was now a shadow of her former self. Yet, from time to time, she did allow herself to imagine what life would be like free from the shackles which confined her to this miserable existence, dictated by her overbearing husband. She had become a subservient automaton devoid of any personality.

When her husband deigned to make an appearance, Evelyn put his breakfast in front of him without demurring. It was just part of the daily ritual which had evolved over the years. After Horry had finished his breakfast, he settled down to read the newspaper for an hour or so.

'Right, time to fix the aerial, I think, before it starts to rain. I'll get the ladder in position first,' said Horry, as he got up and went out the door.

After putting it up against the gable end, he went back into the house, switched on the television and opened the window.

'Right, blockhead, can you remember what you've got to do? You look at the screen and when you see a picture, you shout out to let me know, got it? Why do I know this is going to go wrong? Honestly, it would be easier and quicker to train a chimp.'

Evelyn stood stoically as Horry denigrated her once again. As he went out, she turned to look at the television, and all was quiet. Then, a few minutes later, there came a loud scream-cum-shout followed by a sickening thud and the clatter of the ladder landing on the patio.

Evelyn looked to the window then casually walked out of the house, picking up a cloth as she went. When she got outside, she looked down at her husband, whose head was lying in a pool of blood. It was self-evident he was dead. A sanctimonious smile crept across her face as she nonchalantly wiped the grease from the feet of the ladder.

Heads I Win, Tails You Lose

The unrelenting heat of the sun was beating down on Annabel as she stood poised on the brink of success. All the practise and dedication would now culminate in the next few minutes. She took slow, controlled breaths, conscious that all eyes were focused on her. The silence heightened the tension. Nervously, she looked up at her opponent and then down at the grass as she bounced the ball. All that was needed was one unreturnable serve and the title would be hers. A quick look up again and then down. Annabel tossed the ball in the air and then followed through with her racquet, putting all her weight behind it. Chalk flew up from the centre line as her opponent desperately scrambled across the base line to try and reach it.

It was an ace.

'Game, set and match, Miss Burlington Smythe. 6-4, 6-

7, 6-4.'

Annabel threw her racquet up in the air and sank to her knees. She'd done it. She was now Norfolk County Women's Singles Champion, and she had managed it before her eighteenth birthday. With sweat running down her face, she closed her eyes and savoured the moment.

To the sound of polite applause, Annabel got to her feet, looked at her parents who were standing and clapping, and gave them a raised fist in triumph. She then looked further along to where her boyfriend, Greg, was watching. His face radiating ear to ear smiles whilst doing fist-pumps. It was such a shame he couldn't have been with her parents. It would have made her day complete.

Annabel walked towards the net to commiserate with her adversary, who had made her fight all the way for victory.

'Well played,' said Annabel, as they air-kissed. 'It could have gone either way.'

'You've only got the cup on loan,' she replied with a smile. 'I shall be back next year for revenge.'

'Bring it on, sister!'

After the presentation and photographs, Greg was waiting impatiently for Annabel in order to congratulate her. 'Well done. You were brilliant,' he said. 'You actually did it! What's next? Wimbledon?'

'I hardly think so. I'm a long way off that standard.'

'But even Serena Williams had to start somewhere. You need to set your sights high,' said Greg. 'I've always dreamed of being married to a Grand Slam winner.'

'And that's all it will ever be – a dream – if I've got anything to do with it. Annabel is going places and she won't be able to do that if she's tied to you.'

Greg knew who that was before he turned around: it was Annabel's father, Sir Clifford.

'Oh, er… hello Sir Clifford. I was just saying how well Annabel played.'

'Please don't do this now, Daddy. Don't spoil the day for me.'

'This wastrel has spoilt the day for me by being here and collaring my daughter.'

'Now, now, Clifford dear, let's not do this here, remember where you are,' said his wife, Lady Patricia.

'Very well,' he said, looking daggers at Greg. 'Come along Annabel, we are going home to celebrate your success with a bottle or two of Pol Roger.'

Annabel turned to a dejected Greg and said, 'Sorry about that.'

'It's not your fault, and I'm getting used to it, anyway.'

'It won't always be like this. I'm eighteen next weekend and I'll be free as a bird to do what I like. I'll call you later, and thanks for coming.

'You really could do much better for yourself than Greg

Chambers, you know,' said Sir Clifford, on the journey back.

'I don't understand what you've got against him,' replied Annabel. 'He's honest, trustworthy, kind and thoughtful.'

'But he's not going anywhere, is he? What are his prospects for the future? How is he going to be able to provide for you? Let's face it, he's not one of us.'

'You're such a supercilious snob. Okay, he comes from a different background but that doesn't make him any less of a person.'

'Just remind me again, what is it he does for a living?'

'He's a cabinet maker.'

'Ah, yes, a cabinet maker. Not very cerebral, is it?

Just because Greg uses his hands, it doesn't mean he's not intelligent. He is very well-read and he also writes,' said Annabel.

'Yes, my dear. I'm sure Greg is quite charming in his own way,' said Lady Patricia. 'But you have to look at it in the long term. Where is he going?'

'Who knows what the future holds? Greg is not given to fanciful pipe-dreams. But there will always be a need for traditional, highly-skilled cabinet makers; they are at a premium. But that doesn't matter as long as we're happy – and we are.'

'It's all very well having these ideologies when you're young but you'll find things are very different in the big, wide world,' said Sir Clifford.

'Why are you so money-orientated all the time? It is possible to be happy without money, you know.'

'Said the girl whose father has given her everything.'

'You'll see soon enough,' said Annabel.

'And what's that supposed to mean?' he replied.

'I'll be eighteen next Saturday, and I won't need your permission for anything.'

'Please don't tell me you're planning to go off and marry that plebeian. If you do, I'll tell you now, I will disinherit you, even if you are my only child. You will not get so much as a penny from me. It will be goodbye to Apsley Hall and its contents, and my money, as well.'

'Really, Clifford; that's going a bit too far. Take no notice dear, your father didn't mean it.'

'Didn't I?'

'Whatever,' said Annabel, and went back to looking at the scenery in silence for the rest of the journey. The jubilation of her win that day, now seemed like a brief moment of joy from the distant past. Why couldn't he just be happy for me? she thought. Greg was a good, sensible person, who never got into any trouble, not so much as a parking ticket. But because he didn't come from *"good stock"* and he didn't have a high-flying job, her father thought Greg was out to get his hands on his fortune. Annabel thought no one, short of a prince, would ever be good enough for her in her father's eyes.

'Hello, love. How did Annabel get on?'

'She won,' said Greg with a smile. 'But her obnoxious father put a bit of a damper on things.'

'Usual stuff, was it?' said his mother. 'You not being good enough for his daughter?'

'Yeah, something like that.'

'Was Lady Patricia there?'

'Yeah, but she's very much in his shadow – not saying much. I do believe, given time, we could win her over, but it will never happen with her father. He's had a lifetime of getting whatever he wants and he doesn't care what he has to do to get it, or who he has to trample over. His sort always seems to come out on top.'

'Do you see your relationship doomed, then?'

'No, not necessarily. Annabel is her own person.'

'But what if it came to a choice between you and her family? How would you see that panning out?'

'Good question. Hopefully, it won't come to that but we'll find out next weekend.'

'What do you mean? What are you planning?'

'Sorry, Mum, I'd rather not say at the moment.'

His mother knew that steely look in his eyes: the same as his father had – one of determination. He had obviously made up his mind about something. 'Are you planning to force Sir Clifford's hand, by any chance? It could all end in tears, you know.'

'Please, just leave it for now, Mum.'

'At least promise me you won't do anything rash.'

'As if,' he said with a grin.

'So, what are your plans for this evening? Are you seeing Annabel?'

'No, not tonight. According to her father, they are going to celebrate her win, but I will speak to her later. Right, I'm going to grab a shower before dinner, if that's alright?'

'Yes, okay. Dinner will be about half-an-hour.'

That evening, Greg was immersed in the latest Ian Rankin novel when his mobile rang. He picked it up and saw it was Annabel. 'Well, hello, Annabel Burlington Smythe, doyen of the centre court.'

'I wish,' she said.

'How did the celebrations go?'

'I left after the first drink and went to my room. Daddy started going on about you, as per usual. I just can't get through to him. He doesn't seem to realise that all he's doing is making me more determined. I mean, he only wanted to stop you coming to my party next Saturday.'

'What did you say?'

'I told him if you weren't there, then neither would I be. That shut him up. I do so hope he doesn't spoil the evening by causing a scene in front of all my friends and relations.'

'He wouldn't do that, would he? He likes to present himself as being the all- round, benevolent, good guy. I'm sure he wouldn't want people to see the other side of him. The bullying ogre to any unfortunate who doesn't agree with his diktats.'

'Yes, I think you're right. His image – his personae – is very important to him. He likes to be seen in a favourable light, be it friend or foe. It's important he presents the image he wants others to see, as you know well enough.'

'He'll never come between us, will he?' said Greg.

'No, not if I've got anything to do with it.'

'That's good to hear. I couldn't bear it if he were to drive us apart.'

'How's the book coming along?' asked Annabel, changing the subject. 'When can I read it?'

'When it's finished.'

'When will that be?'

'I don't know. It takes a long time, especially when you've got a full-time job to hold down, as well. Some authors take years to complete a book. It's not as easy as you might think. It takes a lot of hard work to write a book that's easy to read.'

'When it's finished, I'm sure Daddy would like a signed copy for his library,' she said, with mock sincerity.

'Yeah, right.'

'Maybe he'll see you in a different light if you manage to get it published.'

'And maybe he'll provide me with a dowry, as well, when we get married,' added Greg, with equal insouciance.

'I think we're getting a bit ahead of ourselves, aren't we? We've gone from you being a bestselling author to being married with half-a-dozen children, and all with the benevolence of my father.'

'Okay, so maybe me being an author was a tad over-ambitious, but everything else is doable, isn't it?'

'Oh, but of course, my dear – indubitably,' she said, as she laughed at the absurdity of it all.

'And we missed out the bit about when you become a grand slam winner and the millions start rolling in.'

'Yes, we'd become *the* in vogue, celebrity couple of the day.'

'Heaven forbid,' said Greg, a shiver of dread going down his spine at the very thought of it.

* * *

Saturday dawned bright and sunny as Annabel drew back the curtains and surveyed the manicured grounds to the rear of Apsley Hall. A marquee had been erected in readiness for her birthday bash that evening. She was happy and excited by the prospect of what the day might have in store. Tonight, there would be somewhere in the region of two hundred guests attending. Her parents had spared no expense in organizing a lavish party for her. There would be something for everyone to enjoy no matter what their taste might be.

Having showered, Annabel was getting dressed when her phone rang; she knew who it would be. 'Hello, Birthday Girl speaking. All gifts graciously received.'

'Happy birthday, darling.'

'Thank you, Greg. I knew you'd be the first to call. I'm so looking forward to the day ahead.'

'Have you had any surprises, yet?'

'No, but I'm now about to go down to breakfast, so there might be something in store for me. I've got absolutely no idea what Mummy and Daddy have bought me.'

'Okay, you best go down and find out. So, what time do you want to see me tonight?'

'Guests will start arriving about seven-thirty, but you can come before then.'

'What about your father? I can't imagine he'd be too pleased to see me arrive early, like I was one of the family. He would be less likely to kick-off if I arrived with the other guests.'

'You may well have a point. I'll leave it up to you as long as you make sure you do come.'

'You try stopping me – or your father.'

'That's the spirit. See you later. Byeee.'

Annabel went down to breakfast and found her parents

had already started.

'Happy birthday, darling,' they chorused.

'Here, have some Bucks Fizz,' said her father, pouring her a glass. 'Now you're legally entitled to drink it.'

'Cheers,' said Annabel, picking up her glass. 'Here's to a happy birthday with no hiccups.'

'Eat your breakfast first, darling, then you can have your present,' said her mother.

'What is it? Where is it?' said an excited Annabel, looking around.

'All in good time, dear. All in good time. It all comes to he – or in this case, she – who waits,' said her proud, smiling father. 'And I'm confident you'll find it was worth waiting for.'

'You're such a tease, Daddy. I think you get a perverse kind of pleasure from doing it. You play me in much the same way you play a salmon when you're fishing.'

'It's one of life's great pleasures.'

'Oh, come on, Daddy, please don't keep me in suspense.'

'Very well, then.' He picked up an envelope and handed it to her. 'It's a card from your mother and me.'

'Thank you. Is the present inside?' she said, thinking it might be a cheque.

'Open it and see.'

Annabel quickly opened it and pulled out a beautiful card. Inside was written: *Happy 18th birthday to the most wonderful and beautiful daughter we could have wished for. We are so proud of you.* And there was a small key stuck to the card.

'Thank you for those lovely words…er, what's the key for?'

'Aha,' said her father, getting up and opening the cupboard door of a dresser and taking out a gift-wrapped parcel and placing it in front of her.

'What is it? It feels like a wooden box.'

'Why don't you open it and find out?' said her mother.

Annabel carefully untied all the ribbons and bows before gently sliding her fingers under the gift-wrap to reveal an exquisite satinwood box with inlaid marquetry of tulipwood, rosewood and kingwood. In the centre of the lid was a cartouche which was inscribed with her name and the day's date.

'Wow, it's absolutely beautiful – a work of art. I shall treasure it forever. Is there anything inside?' she said, trying to lift up the lid. 'Oh, it's locked…ah, I get it – the key. That's what the key is for.'

Annabel turned the key in the lock and gingerly lifted the lid, peering in with the expectation of finding something inside. With her eyes open wide and eyebrows raised, she reached into the box and then frowned as she brought out a black velvet blindfold. 'What the…Are you still playing games with me, Daddy?'

'Who? Me? Now would I do such a thing?'

'Yes, you would. What does it mean, Mummy? What's it for?'

'What do you think a blindfold is for?' she replied.

'Yes, I know, but…Oh, come on…I don't understand.'

'Maybe if you put it on, you'll find out.'

'Have you got me another present – is that it?'

'Put the blindfold on!' said her parents, in unison.

'Okay. Okay, I'm doing it,' she said, putting it on.

'Now stand up,' her father said. 'We are going for a short walk. I will guide you.'

Annabel took small, hesitant steps as she was disorientated by the darkness. Her father's hands on her shoulders guided her through the labyrinth of doors and into the reception hall. He stopped her and said, 'I'll just open the front door. Take a couple more steps. That's it. You can now remove the blindfold.'

'Wooow! That's—That's absolutely brilliant. How can I ever thank you? It is mine, isn't it?' said Annabel, turning to embrace her parents. 'Thank you. Thank you. Thank you.'

She turned round again to look at the brand-new, shiny, red Mini Cooper S, which had a large ribbon wrapped around it with a bow on the top. 'I can't wait to test-drive it, but first I'm going to take a photo of it to send to all my friends – they'll be green with envy.'

'What time are you leaving, Greg?' his mother asked.

'I've got a taxi booked for seven.'

'So, you've got time for a bite to eat beforehand?'

'No thanks Mum, there'll be plenty of food at the party.'

'You still haven't told me what you've bought Annabel. Is it a secret?'

'Yes, I'm afraid it is for now. I'll tell you tomorrow.'

'Will you take this and give it to Annabel. It's just a little something from me,' she said, handing him a gift-wrapped parcel.

'Oh, how sweet of you. I'm sure she'll appreciate it. What is it?'

'I can't tell you, it's a secret. I'll tell you tomorrow.'

'Touché,' said Greg smiling.

When Greg arrived at Apsley Hall, there were about fifty or so guests there already. He looked around for Annabel and saw her emerging from the marquee; she looked absolutely stunning. Her blonde hair neatly framed her face and then tumbled down, resting on her shoulders. She was wearing a black Alexander McQueen, high neck, sleeveless, crepe gown. She turned her head from side to side as if she was looking for someone or something. When her eyes came to rest on Greg, she made a beeline for him, her face wreathed in smiles. They kissed, and Greg held her at arm's length and looked her up and down, surveying the vision of beauty before him.

'You look amazing,' he said.

'Thank you, it's nice to know my effort is appreciated. Here we go, have a glass of bubbly,' said Annabel, grabbing two glasses from the tray of a passing waiter.

'Cheers! Happy birthday. And here's to a happy, enjoyable evening, and wishing you good health and happiness.'

'Thank you. Cheers.'

'Oh, mother gave me this to give to you,' he said, handing her the gift.

'How kind of her. Would you be a sweetie and put it on the table in the garden room with the others, please?'

'Yeah, sure. I've got something for you for later.'

'Ooh, I look forward to that. Listen, I'm going to have to leave you for now, I have to meet and greet, but there'll be people here – friends – who you'll know. And I'm really pleased that you're here: it wouldn't have been the same without you.'

'You say the sweetest of things.'

'But only to the sweetest of people!' And with that, she was gone.

Greg wandered around the grounds, stopping to chat to various friends and acquaintances whilst he waited for Annabel to join him. The numbers were beginning to swell and there was a general hubbub as people talked animatedly in their groups. There was a feeling of *joie de vivre* about the evening – a warm conviviality. It was just as it should be, he thought.

Greg walked into the huge marquee and looked around. At one end there was a stage where the band had set up their equipment for later. A DJ was playing ambient background music as people took seats at the tables situated along the sides of the marquee, leaving space for people to dance.

'There you are,' came a voice from behind. Greg turned to be greeted with an effervescent smile from Annabel. 'Right – duties done – I'm all yours. Let's refresh our glasses.'

'You couldn't have asked for a better evening for the party,' said Greg, as they made their way to the pop-up champagne bar.

'No, everything is going nicely. Even Daddy is in a good mood.'

'Really? That augurs well for us, then.'

'What do you mean?'

'Well, he may not cause a contretemps should we come face to face.'

'I'm sure he wouldn't – not this evening.'

They had their glasses replenished and strolled around the garden, stopping to chat with guests. There was a fire-eater wandering around doing spontaneous demonstrations of his art. Also, a conjuror was moving from group to group doing close-up magic, drawing gasps of amazement and incredulity from the onlookers.

'Are you getting peckish, yet?' asked Annabel.

'Yes,' he replied 'I haven't eaten since lunch.'

'Okay, let's head to the marquee and get a seat; the buffet should be ready soon.'

They stood just inside the marquee, and Annabel said, 'Right, we need more drinks.'

'Steady on, I've had four already,' said Greg.

'Who's counting?'

'I am. I don't want to get drunk and spoil the evening. Think what your father would have to say.'

'His mind is made up, anyway.'

'Yes, but if we're to stand any chance of winning him round, I don't want to blot my copy book any further.'

'I suppose we could try testing the water.'

'What do you mean?' said Greg.

'Well, Daddy has been knocking them back since before the guests arrived. He's not squiffy, or anything, but he's more relaxed and might be a bit more receptive.'

'What are you suggesting?'

'How about we get another drink and then go and sit at his table, ready for the food?'

'Are you serious? How many have you had?'

'I'm perfectly serious. He's never going to make the first move to try and get to know you, is he? So, let's have a face-off.'

Greg thought about it. He could see the logic behind her thinking, but he didn't want to risk a once-and-for-all, out-of-hand rejection. But Annabel was right, her father would never make a move in that direction and this opportunity may never present itself again.

'Okay, I'm willing to give it a try, but you do realise he could make a scene and ruin the evening for you?'

'No, no. There's safety in numbers. He won't say anything with so many people around. Come on, let's go.'

Seated at the table were Sir Clifford, Lady Patricia, the local MP, Ian Waddlestone and his wife, Elspeth, plus the High Sheriff, Penelope Rainsford and her spouse, George.

We should be safe in this august company, thought Greg, as he slowly eased himself onto the chair between Annabel and the MP.

'Of course, you know my daughter, Annabel, don't you?' said Sir Clifford. 'And that's, er…her…hurrumph.'

'I'm Greg,' he volunteered, in what he hoped was a calm and confident manner. 'Annabel's boyfriend.'

So far, so good, thought Greg, purposefully avoiding eye contact with Sir Clifford. He consciously felt himself relax a little, having introduced himself. And it passed without any vitriol from Annabel's father, just as she said it would. Conversation resumed around the table and Greg turned to Annabel, who smiled at him and gave a slight nod in recognition of what he'd done.

He was over the first hurdle.

Having eaten, and drunk another two glasses from the

bottles in the centre of the table, Greg was gaining in confidence. He was striking up conversation with the great and the good, but not Sir Clifford, who he caught glaring at him on a couple of occasions. Annabel was admiring the way Greg was handling himself with the dignitaries, she felt quite proud of him.

With the others around the table engaged in conversation, Greg thought it was as good a time as any.

'We really ought to go and mingle,' said Annabel.

'Oh, yes, of course. But before we do, I, er—there's something—I mean, will you—that is to say…' Greg struggled to get the words out as he fumbled in his pocket. Finally, his hand came out clutching a small box, which he proceeded to open, revealing a blue sapphire and diamond ring.

'Oh, Greg…'

'What the hell do you think you're doing, BOY?' boomed Sir Clifford.

The table went quiet as all eyes switched to Sir Clifford then across to Annabel and Greg.

'Daddy please don't—'

'My God, you've got a brass neck on you. How dare you be so presumptuous? I forbid it, do you hear? I forbid it!'

An indignant Greg, turned to Sir Clifford and said, 'I think, sir, you'll find it's for Annabel to decide.'

'Daddy, don't do this.'

'I've warned you what will happen if you go ahead: I will disinherit you.'

'Look, Daddy, we are going ahead with this. We would prefer to do it with your blessing but, if needs be, we'll do it without.'

'Clifford,' whispered Lady Patricia, pulling at his sleeve. 'You're embarrassing yourself and them. Just remember where you are. Why not give them a chance? Otherwise, you're going to lose Annabel forever.'

'I, er…,' Sir Clifford gave a nervous little laugh as he was brought back to the here and now, conscious of what his guests were listening to. After some thought he said, 'I, er— well, young man, I'm prepared to give you a sporting chance. I'll take two pieces of paper and on one I shall write *"marry"* and on the other I shall write *"separate"*. I will screw them up and put them in this bowl. You will choose one and whatever it says, that will be what happens. Do you agree?'

'Daddy, no. You can't do this to us, it's not fair.'

'It's okay, Annabel,' said Greg. 'It will be fine. Stick with me.'

'How do we know we can trust you?' said Annabel.

'Of course, you can trust me, I'm your father, and I am a man of my word. And we have witnesses here to see fair play.'

'Look, we've got nothing to lose and everything to gain,' said Greg, squeezing her hand.

'But...'

'Very well, sir, I accept the wager.'

'Good lad.'

Sir Clifford wrote on two pieces of paper, then screwed them up into balls and placed them in the bowl, giving it a good shake before placing it in the centre of the table. 'Over to you, young man,' he said, fixing Greg with a firm, confident stare.

Annabel and Greg looked at each other. Annabel showing visible signs of the tension. This was all wrong. There was a lot at stake. With all eyes on him, Greg reached into the bowl and swilled the balls around before pulling one of them out. He looked at Sir Clifford and held his gaze; the piece of paper in his hand. Greg could see the corners of Sir Clifford's mouth gradually turn upwards in a smug, self-satisfied manner. A quick look at Annabel, who was finding the tension unbearable. She looked at him beseechingly, hoping lady luck was on their side. There was complete silence as he slowly unravelled the piece of paper. He looked at it, then looked Sir Clifford in the eye and promptly put the paper in his mouth and swallowed it. There was a sharp intake of breath but the silence still prevailed.

Greg was giving nothing away.

After what seemed like hours, but was in fact only seven or eight seconds, Lady Patricia broke the silence. 'What was on the piece of paper?'

Greg looked Sir Clifford in the eye once again and said, 'marry.' He continued to stare unblinking into Sir Clifford's eyes, daring him to challenge it. Very gradually, Sir Clifford's eyes began to narrow and a scowl formed on his face as the penny dropped. He had worked out what Greg had done, and there was nothing he could do about it.

'I guess congratulations are in order, then,' said Lady Patricia. 'What do you say, Clifford?'

'Well, er, yes, but of course,' he said, putting on a false smile for the benefit of those around the table.

'Thank you, Daddy, you won't regret it, I promise. Everything will work out fine. You've made me very happy.'

'And that's all that matters,' he said ruefully.

'Come on, Greg, I want to tell all my friends and show them my gorgeous ring.'

When they got outside, Annabel threw her arms around him as tears of happiness rolled down her face. 'Don't you ever put me through anything else like that; it was too much of a gamble.'

'No, it wasn't.'

'What? It could easily have gone the other way.'

'No, it couldn't'

'Why? What are you saying?'

'I knew your father wouldn't play fair, so I took him on at his own game.'

'What do you mean?'

'Your father wrote *"separate"* on both pieces of paper to make sure he would win whichever one I chose.'

'But you claimed it said *"marry",* and why did you swallow it?'

'The paper I drew said *"separate"* so I swallowed it before anyone could see it and prove me wrong. The remaining paper also had *"separate"* on it. So, to all intents and purposes, the paper I drew must have had *"marry"* on it. Your father couldn't have said any different without losing credibility in front of his distinguished guests. Simple.'

'There's nothing simple about you, Greg Chambers. You were more than a match for my father. However, you still haven't actually proposed to me yet!'

Food for Thought

Albert Mullins was a creature of habit, an advocate for routine and tradition. He was also a stickler for rules and regulations. Every morning, he would leave his house at 9:20 precisely and walk to work, arriving at the library at 9:43 to let the staff in. Albert had followed this routine for the past 42 years, 25, of which, as Head Librarian.

His first job was to walk up and down the aisles checking the books were neat and tidy on the shelves, before opening up at 10 o'clock. He would then retire to his office, where he would remain largely undisturbed for most of the day unless there was a problem. At 11 o'clock, one of the staff would bring him a cup of coffee and a biscuit. This was repeated at 1 o'clock and 3:30. At the end of the day, Albert would do his security round, checking doors and windows were secured. Then, at 6:15, he would set off for home, arriving at 6:38.

Albert had never married; well, if the truth be known,

he had never had a girlfriend. He was an only child, who had lived with his parents until they passed away, and he had now been living on his own, in the house, for nearly five years. On the first Sunday of the month, he would dutifully tend his parents' graves, weather permitting.

So, now, when he got home from work, he had to cook his own dinner, having prepared everything in the morning before he left the house. Albert would also set the table in readiness for the meal, which he liked to have at 7:45. So, with everything under control, he would pour himself a glass of sherry to enjoy before having his dinner.

There was a lot to be said for careful planning and timing; you knew exactly where you were and what you're supposed to be doing. This led to less confusion and uncertainty; things ran smoothly and efficiently.

Albert shied away from confrontation, but that's not to say he wasn't insistent that correct protocol should be observed. He had ways of ensuring things were done in a timely manner, and would take steps to seek redress if he had to.

So, it was an orderly world that Albert Mullins inhabited, which extended to include his annual holiday. Every year, without fail, he would go to the Lake District. Which was why he was in a particularly good mood that day. Tomorrow he was off on his sojourn to the Land of the Lakes.

At 3:30, Frances brought him his coffee and biscuit. 'It

won't be long now, Mr. Mullins; this time tomorrow you'll be in the Lakes – I do envy you.'

'Yes,' said Albert, 'I am really looking forward to it: a chance to relax and get some fresh, country air, surrounded by beautiful scenery.'

'Have you ever given any thought to moving there when you retire?'

Retiring was something he had thought about a lot recently. He was dreading it: the end of his daily routine. He would be surplus to requirements, no longer of any use. In short, he would be lost. The library had been his *raison d'etre* for the past 40-odd-years. It wouldn't survive without him.

'I haven't got any plans at the moment, Frances, but it's certainly an idea worth thinking about.'

'You would find plenty of inspiration for writing your poetry. You know, when you *"wander lonely as a cloud."* It worked for him.'

'Quite, but I wouldn't put myself in the same category.'

'Well, I hope you enjoy yourself and don't forget your waterproofs; they have been known to have the odd shower or two up there.'

That evening, Albert had a spring in his step as he walked home: he was really looking forward to tomorrow. He stopped off at the off-licence to buy a bottle of Gonzalez Byass, his favourite sherry, to take with him on holiday. That meant he didn't arrive home until 6:47, but, for once, he didn't care. Albert was buoyed with an overwhelming sense of *joie de vivre.*

* * *

The following morning, his taxi arrived at 9:15 to take him on the first leg of his journey to Peterborough station. There, he caught the 10:30 train to Windermere, a journey time of five hours and fifty-four minutes, with a change at Manchester Piccadilly. Albert liked travelling by train; watching the little vignettes of daily life played out as the train flashed past. He never grew tired of the ever-changing panorama, there was always something different to see. Sometimes he would find his mind wandering as he was transported to some faraway place. So, before he knew it, the train pulled into Windermere station. Albert checked his watch, 4:26, only two minutes late – not bad.

Outside the station, he commandeered a taxi to take him to the Lakeside Guesthouse, where he always stayed. On ringing the doorbell, it was answered by a well-dressed woman in her sixties.

'Hello Mr. Mullins, how nice to see you again. Do come in.'

'Thank you Mrs. Battersby, and it's nice to see you too.'

'I've prepared your usual room; I'll get Roger to carry your case up for you.'

'No, no, it's okay. I can manage.'

'Are you sure? It's no trouble.'

'No, really.'

'Okay, I'll show you up to your room.'

When they entered the room Mrs. Battersby said, 'I think you'll find everything is in order, let me know if there's anything else you require. I've put a schooner on the bedside table for you, I know how much you enjoy a tipple before dinner. I take it you brought a bottle of sherry with you?'

'Yes, thank you, you're very kind.'

'Right, I'll leave you to unpack, dinner is at 6:30 as usual. See you later.'

Albert unpacked his case, putting his prized Gonzalez Byass beside the glass Mrs. Battersby had thoughtfully provided. It was a shame they didn't have a licence, but he didn't mind bringing his own. He checked his watch: 5:35, there was time to take a shower and change before dinner.

Suitably refreshed, Albert sat in a chair to look out of the window at the view of the lake, and partook of a small libation before going down to dinner.

He enjoyed the chicken chasseur, but what made it even better, was the fact, he didn't have to prepare and cook it, or do the washing up afterwards – a welcome change.

* * *

The following day, Albert wandered around Windermere, doing some window shopping. He wasn't fussed about going inside the shops, though he did make an exception when it came to bookshops. After a light lunch in a café, he decided to take a boat trip around the lake. There was something relaxing and calming about water.

At 5:15 Albert found himself back at the guesthouse with plenty of time to shower and change. It had been a nice, relaxing day, and after he had showered, he poured himself a glass of sherry and sat down to wait for dinner. Very civilized.

* * *

The next day, Albert caught a bus to Grasmere, a distance of eight miles or so. He wanted to go to Dove Cottage where Wordsworth had lived. He thought maybe he might gain some inspiration if he was to immerse himself in the surroundings of the great man.

After spending some time in the cottage, Albert went to the lake and hired a rowing boat to take himself to the island in the middle. There, he sat and ate the packed lunch Mrs. Battersby had made for him, before getting down to the serious business of composing a poem.

An hour passed by and Albert put his pad down, he had only written two lines, obviously the creative juices weren't flowing today. So much for getting Wordsworth's influence to rub off on him. Eventually, he got back in the boat and rowed to the shore, and then took a leisurely stroll to the bus stop.

When he got back to the guesthouse, he followed his usual routine of showering and having a glass of sherry. Albert continued with this pattern over the next couple of days; going to Hill Top, at Near Sawrey, where Beatrix Potter had lived, then walking along Esthwaite Water to Hawkshead. And the next day, going on an excursion to Keswick.

When he returned from Keswick, Albert had a shower as usual, and when he went to pour himself a sherry, he thought the level in the bottle had gone down since the evening before. Surely not; nobody would have helped themselves, would they? he thought. Albert poured a glass and put the bottle down, then marked the level of the sherry on the bottle. Now he would be able to check if somebody had helped themselves again.

* * *

The following morning, over breakfast, Albert gave some thought to what Frances, his assistant, had said about retiring there. It was very appealing; he loved the landscape which was so inspiring of writers and artists. It offered respite from the rigours of modern-day life. A chance to be at one with nature, away from the hustle and bustle. He thought it wouldn't do any harm to investigate the property market whilst he was there. So that was what

Albert did that day: he went to see what the estate agents had to offer.

It was in a somewhat buoyant mood that he returned to the guesthouse. There were a few cottages within his price range in the Ambleside area, which he favoured. So, yes, it would be doable when the time comes, should he make that decision.

Albert had his shower and dressed, and when he went to pour his customary glass of sherry, he noticed the level in the bottle was now below his mark. He was fuming, somebody was helping themselves, but who? Now Albert was not one to cause a scene and he didn't like confrontation, so he had to think carefully about what he was going to do. Somebody was going to pay for this. Albert poured himself a glass and then proceeded to pee in the bottle and then make another mark. Whoever was helping themselves would rue the day; nobody was going to get the better of him.

* * *

The next evening, when Albert went to his room, the first thing he did was check the bottle. A wide grin spread across his face: the level had gone down again.

At dinner, he studied the other guests to see if there were any signs of someone having drunk his sherry, but everyone seemed to be fine.

Albert was finishing his coffee in the dining room as Mrs. Battersby was clearing the tables.

'Did you enjoy your meal Mr. Mullins?'

'Yes, thank you.'

'I take it trifle must be your favourite; I noticed you are the only one to have it every night.'

'Yes; I must say, you make a delicious trifle.'

'Thank you. I'm afraid I have a bit of a confession to make; I hope you don't mind, but I ran out of sherry, so I borrowed some of yours to put in the trifle.'

Lost and Found

As the last vestiges of the summer sun penetrated the wispy, white clouds, Cassie was strolling along Cromer pier. It was September and most of the holidaymakers had gone, leaving the town in relative peace once more. She loved coming here at this time of year, when it was not so busy. There was something quintessentially English about taking a leisurely stroll along the pier. Cassie imagined what it must have been like in the Victorian era. The ladies in their long dresses, holding their parasols and the gentlemen in their Sunday best, complete with top hat and cane. Cassie was dressed in jeans and a fleece plus the obligatory trainers, which were *de rigueur* for the younger generation, though she was fast approaching her sixties.

The breeze had a salty tang which was somehow invigorating, giving a certain *frisson* to the experience.

She stopped and leaned on the rail, watching the anglers trying to catch something for their tea. As Cassie looked out across the sea, there were a few windsurfers doing battle with the elements. It looked quite exhilarating as they suddenly caught the wind in their sail and accelerated at a great number of knots. She quite fancied having a go, but she was reticent when it came to mixing with people.

Cassie walked down the side of the pavilion and round the back, where the lifeboat was stationed, before coming back, full circle, to the front. As she walked along, she could feel the sea-breeze which was a bit cool, so she sat on a bench which was sheltered from the wind. Seated at the other end was an elderly lady reading a book. After a while, she put her book down and turned to face Cassie.

'Nice day.'

'Er, yes, it is,' replied Cassie. 'The sun is lovely when you get out of the wind.'

'It was built in 1822.'

'What was?'

'The pier,' said the lady.

Cassie looked at her and saw a wearied face which gave credence to the fact she'd had a hard life. Her sallow complexion made her look gaunt, and, yet, there was a glimmer of a spark in her expectant eyes. She was alive within, but at the same time Cassie detected a hint of sadness. And sadness was something she knew a lot about.

‘I didn’t realize it was that old. I imagine it could tell a few tales about secret assignations and suchlike.’

‘Yes, no doubt it could.’

‘It’s a perfect place to come if you want to be alone with your thoughts and reflect on life.’

‘Is that what you’re doing? I’ve seen you a few times, here on the pier, looking somewhat sad and lost.’

Oh dear, what am I doing, thought Cassie, getting drawn into conversation with a stranger? ‘I, er, I’m a…I’m sorry, I’m afraid I have to go,’ she said, hastily getting to her feet. ‘It was nice to meet you. Goodbye.’

‘I’m sorry, have I said something?’

‘No, no. It’s a…I mean, er…I must go, sorry.’

‘Hope to see you again,’ the lady called out, as Cassie headed off at a brisk pace.

* * *

As the following day dawned, Cassie got out of bed and made herself some breakfast, temporarily forgetting what day it was. Drinking her coffee, it came back to her and she reflected on what it meant. Well, it didn’t mean anything, did it? Not now. It was just another day. But a day which reinforced – heightened – the sadness and loneliness which had dogged her unremittingly for so many years. So how could she spend the day? Going back to the pier would bring back memories of happier times which would inevitably be tinged with sadness, too. There didn't appear to be an easy answer, but the pier held an attraction for her, so it wasn't surprising that she found herself heading in that direction later that morning.

Stepping onto the pier, Cassie tried to fill her head with positive, happy thoughts. It was going to be another beautiful day, weather wise. The sun was shining once again and the cool wind had dropped. As she sauntered along, her thoughts turned to the possibility of, maybe, moving to Cromer. She loved the north Norfolk coastal area, which held so many happy memories for her. There was nothing now to keep her in London, so it would make sense to relocate and have a better quality of life. A life lived at a gentle pace with fresh air coursing through her lungs. It wouldn't do any harm to have a look in the estate agents' while she was here.

Cassie now felt buoyed by the prospect of moving to the area. Yes, she should have done it years ago. She hadn't felt like this in a long time: it put a spring in her step. She followed her usual anti-clockwise path around the pavilion, giving the anglers a cursory glance as she passed by. The old lady wasn't sitting on the bench today, so she sat down to give her mind carte blanche to explore the exciting prospect of moving.

As she sat there thinking, her mind began to wander back to the sad times which subsequently – inevitably –

followed the halcyon days of her earlier life. Very soon, before she knew it, she succumbed to the dark clouds which were forming. Cassie now felt overwhelmed by these thoughts as she went into a downward spiral. Would she ever be free from the torment?

'Hello again.'

Cassie looked up to see the elderly lady whom she had spoken to the day before. She felt so down that her anxiety didn't kick in. 'Oh, hello,' she said, in a dull, flat tone.

'What's the matter? You look really down in the dumps.'

'Yeah, well…'

'Would it help to talk about it? I'm a good listener. I'm Rose, by the way.'

'Cassandra, but people call me Cassie.'

'Well now, Cassie, care to tell me what's troubling you?'

She let out a long, audible sigh. 'I dunno, I guess it's just life, really.'

'What about it?'

'Being dealt a crap hand.'

'How so?'

'The wheels of good fortune and fate conspired against me.'

'Oh, dear,' said Rose. 'In what way?'

Cassie stared down at the floor and shook her head as

another heavy sigh escaped. 'It's a long story and I'm sure you don't want to be bored by it.'

'On the contrary: I'd like to hear it, and it might do you some good to get it off your chest. Is there a particular reason why you should feel this way today?'

Whatever am I doing? thought Cassie. I can't let her in, but, then again, she might be right. 'Today is my sixtieth birthday.'

'Happy birthday, Cassie! Surely that's good enough reason to be happy, isn't it?'

'No, it isn't. You see, I am all alone in this world, I've no family and no real friends to help me celebrate. It makes me reflect on the past, to what was and the tragedies that followed.'

'Deary me,' said Rose, 'I'm sorry to hear that, it must be awful for you. Do you want to talk about it?'

Oh well, in for a penny…thought Cassie. 'If you're sure you want to hear it.'

'Yes, I would.'

'Okay. I was born and brought up in the East End of London by my parents, Edward and Anne, and I had a younger brother, David. I had an idyllic childhood. My parents were very loving and supportive. They would help and encourage me in everything I did. Every year we would come here to Cromer for our holidays; I loved it – still do.'

'So, you did have some good times.'

'Oh, yes, I did, that is, until we were driving home after spending a couple of weeks here.'

'What happened?'

'Well, it was raining quite heavily and, as we went round a bend, a lorry jack-knifed across the road and hit us. Our car was buried beneath the trailer and my parents were killed instantly; David died later in hospital. Miraculously, I escaped with cuts and bruises, and very vivid memories of the carnage, which have stayed with me all my life. I was sixteen at the time.'

'Oh, you poor woman, it must have been horrific.'

'Yes, it was, and I've carried the guilt with me ever since.'

'Why should you feel guilty?'

'Because I survived. I should have died with them. Why was I spared? They were my world: all that I had ever known.'

'Maybe you were destined for greater things; as they say, God moves in mysterious ways. So, what happened next?'

'It turned out I had a distant, great aunt on my father's side, who helped me in the aftermath. She dealt with all the formalities and suchlike. I was numb and traumatized at the time, unable to think or do anything. My great aunt took me to stay with her for a while until I felt able to return home, and then…' Cassie's voice trailed off as she thought back to that time, and tears welled up in her eyes.

'It was awful, the house was so quiet and it contained so many reminders. It wasn't that I didn't want those memories, of course I did, but they brought such melancholic sadness, which stayed with me.'

'It's obviously still very raw for you. Did you keep in touch with your great aunt?'

'Kind of. There were regular phone calls to start with but they tailed off after a year or so, and two years later, she died as well. That left me with no relations.'

'How did you manage on your own at such a young age? It must have been difficult.'

'It was at first, but, fortunately, I was well-versed in the skills to run a house. So once I got myself into a routine it worked quite well. I was able to work and run the house. Work was a saving grace for me, it kept my mind occupied, but those lonely evenings…'

'I can empathize with you on the loneliness; I suffer from it myself. But do tell me what's happened since then. Things must have got better for you.'

'Wanna bet?'

'Oh, surely not.'

'Well things did get better,' said Cassie. 'I met and married a wonderful man by the name of Paul. I was blissfully happy, something I hadn't experienced since before the accident. I felt a love I'd never had before – didn't think was possible.'

'How old were you when you got married?'

'I was twenty-eight, and felt as if I had the world at my feet. Life had taken on a whole new meaning for me, we shared many interests and he introduced me to new experiences. We travelled quite a lot and saw something of the world. But no matter where we went, we would always come to Cromer; he grew to love it as well. Paul took me skiing, which was his great passion, and that led directly to another tragedy.'

'Oh, my dear, please don't carry on if it's too painful for you.'

'It's okay: I'm all right,' said Cassie wiping her eyes. 'We went to Austria for a skiing holiday and Paul would spend some time teaching me to ski on the nursery slopes before he went further up the mountain where the experienced skiers went. But that particular day he couldn't resist going off-piste onto virgin snow. He got part-way down when an avalanche started above him, and he wasn't able to outrun it. I watched in horror as the snow engulfed him. The rescuers found his body two days later.

'Once again the bottom dropped out of my world. It seemed as if I was being denied the opportunity to have ever-lasting love and happiness. I really thought we would grow old together. We had so much to live for, but I was a widow at the tender age of thirty-four years.' Cassie sat in silence as the memories flooded back; tears came as she felt the anger well up. How could she have had yet another loved one cruelly snatched away? It just wasn't fair. 'I'm so sorry for this,' she said dabbing her eyes.

'It's perfectly all right, my love, I understand and I'm so sorry you've had so much tragedy in your life. Can I ask if there were any children?'

'No, sadly, we weren't blessed with children; had we been, it would have given me strength – a purpose – to carry on, but as things were, I went into a sharp decline. It was too much for me to cope with on my own. I still keenly felt the loss of my family and it all compounded, and I ended up in hospital for a while. When I came out, I spent a lot of time here convalescing, which gave me time to come to terms with what happened. I eventually went back to work at the bank, where I stayed until I took early retirement five years ago.

'And that's my story; I've been all alone for the past twenty-five years. I've been reluctant to mix with people, a recluse in many respects, afraid to get involved with anyone in case it ended in heartbreak again. Having said that, there's a part of me that wants a relationship. It's so lonely not having anyone to talk to. As a matter of fact, you're the only person I've been able to tell my story to – a complete stranger.'

'I hope I won't be from now on,' said Rose, with a sympathetic smile. 'I haven't had an easy life either, you know. In fact, it's been quite harrowing at times and, like you, I've been very lonely.'

'How come?' said Cassie, going through her pockets for a tissue.

'It all started a long time ago, before you were born. I lived with my parents and sister on the outskirts of Manchester. I was always in trouble with my older parents, who were very strait-laced and God-fearing. I discovered the joy of boys at an early age, and, suffice to say, I found myself pregnant at the age of fifteen.

'Back in those days it was very scandalous, not like it is nowadays. My parents were deeply ashamed and disowned me, telling me to never darken their doorstep again. I was sent packing to this place – an institution – to have the baby, and they told everyone I had gone into service in a big house in London.

'Sadly, when I gave birth, the baby – a girl – was stillborn. I was so overcome by grief, I lost my mind. They thought I was a lunatic and put me in an asylum, where I remained for thirty-two years. That's what happened back in those days.'

'Jeez,' said Cassie, 'did that really happen? That's absolutely awful, to think a young girl could be treated in such an inhumane way. Did you have any contact with the outside world? Did you have visitors?'

'I was forgotten about. I clung on to the forlorn hope my parents would come and get me, but…no, nobody came. Over time, I gradually got better, no thanks to the way I was treated, and I got used to life in the asylum. But it was hell, really, and the conditions were so appalling, you wouldn't keep an animal in them. Obviously, I was released eventually but it was only after an enquiry into why people were being detained for longer than was necessary.'

'So, what happened when you were released? Where did you go?'

'A place was found for me in a hostel – a kind of half-way house – and I had to learn how to cope in a world which was totally alien to me – it was very scary. The trust, which ran the hostel, were very helpful in getting me acquainted with life on the outside. They helped to find me a job in a laundry so I could pay my way. I found it difficult to make friends as I was wary of other people. It was hard for me to trust anyone.

'I never really got used to all the noise – the hustle and bustle – in London. So, I managed, with help, to find a bedsit here in Cromer, which I thought would be a lot quieter and more relaxed. Don't ask me why I chose Cromer, maybe it was because it looked a bit remote, stuck on the coast. I also thought it would give me more of a sense of freedom.'

'You obviously made the right choice, as you're still here after all those years, but what did you do?'

'I was all alone and feeling lonely, so, one day, I decided to try and find my parents and sister, in the hope of a reconciliation. I went to the house where we had lived, just outside of Manchester, only to find somebody else now lived there. I made enquiries at other houses and found Mrs. Dobbs still lived at number forty-one. She told me that my parents had died many years ago, within six months of each other.'

'What about your sister?'

Apparently, she married and moved to London. I did try to trace her but, in London, it's like trying to find a pebble on the beach with a hole in it.'

'So, you've no idea what happened to her, and she obviously never found you.'

'No, and, like you, I've got nobody to share birthdays and Christmas's with.'

'How sad.'

'All I've got is a photograph of my sister and me when we were young. I've got it here in my bag if you'd like to see it.'

'Yes, I would love to.'

'I'm afraid it's a bit dog-eared after all this time; that's me on the left.' A tear rolled down Rose's cheek as she looked at the treasured photograph.

'Oh my God,' said Cassie. 'It can't be…'

'Can't be what?'

'Your sister's name is Anne Briggs, isn't it?'

'Yes, but how on earth did you know that?'

'Your sister is my mother – you're my aunt. I have a

copy of this photo at home. It's surreal…What are the chances of …'

'No. Really?' Rose welled-up again as the reality gradually sank in. 'So, we're not all alone in this world after all.'

As they embraced, the tears flowed and, for once, they were tears of happiness.

A Taste of Honey

There was a long, pregnant pause.

All eyes were firmly fixed on Jessica as she stood beside the swimming pool, dripping wet from head to toe. Her white figure-hugging dress made it transparently obvious she wasn't wearing any underclothes. Some of the assembled party guests were trying hard to suppress the urge to laugh, while others appeared to be somewhat embarrassed.

It was Steve, her husband, who finally broke the silence, giving vent to a hearty, raucous laugh, which was all that was needed for some of the others to join in. Jessica stood, head bowed, biting her bottom lip, trying to force back the tears. Once again, she had fallen victim to one of her husband's practical jokes.

Sarah, the hostess, came quickly to Jessica's aid, wrapping a shawl around her and leading her into the house. At the top of the stairs Sarah indicated a bedroom.

'Go and take your dress off while I get you a towel,' she said.

Jessica entered the tastefully furnished room, and stood looking at her forlorn and bedraggled reflection in the mirror, silently cursing her husband. As she slipped out of her wet dress and let it fall to the floor, Sarah returned, tossing her a towel.

'Here you are. Now let's see if we can find you something to put on.'

'Thanks, you're so kind. I don't know what I would have done without you.'

'That's okay, said Sarah, with a sympathetic smile. 'That's what friends are for, isn't it?'

'Well… yes, I know, but you always seem to be coming to my rescue.'

'I am sure he didn't mean any harm.'

'Like hell he didn't!' blazed Jessica. 'He never stops, and he seems to take particular delight in humiliating me in front of my theatrical friends.'

She dried herself off vigorously, her anger gradually dissipating, and tried on two or three dresses before deciding on a strappy, pale-blue one with a floral print. Then, after attending to her hair and make-up, they both returned to the garden party.

As Jessica picked up a glass of wine, Steve approached her wearing a stupid grin on his face.

'Have a nice dip in the pool?' he asked, with a feigned air of innocence.

She looked daggers at him: she was furious - the anger welling up once more.

'Oh, come on Jess, there's no need to adopt that attitude, it was only a bit of harmless fun.'

'Harmless fun? You call that harmless fun? You never know when to stop, do you? One of these days you'll get your comeuppance – mark my words.' With that, she threw the wine in his face and stormed off.

'What's the matter with you?' he shouted after her. 'Lost your sense of humour?'

The question went unanswered as Jessica got into the car and drove off.

* * *

It took two days and a bouquet of flowers before the frosty atmosphere in the house began to thaw.

'Friends again?' asked Steve. 'All forgiven?'

'Friends. But if you think I'm going to forgive you for what you did you've—'

'Haven't I apologised enough?' he cut in.

'It still doesn't make what you did, right; but let's not go into all that again.'

'Okay,' agreed Steve, thinking, on reflection, it best to let the matter drop. 'Look why don't you go into town and buy yourself a new dress or something for Saturday?'

'Saturday?'

'Yes, Saturday – *Annual Rotary Club Dinner* – remember?'

'Oh, yes, I remember now, that's the only night of the year when us mere women are permitted to enter the bastion of your male dominated society,' she replied, sarcastically.

'Come on Jess, there's no need for all that, you know you always enjoy yourself.'

If she were honest, she didn't particularly enjoy these dinners, but she always made the effort for his sake.

'Where is it being held this year?' she enquired.

'That hotel in Silver Street; the name escapes me.'

'Oh, you mean the King's Head. I believe they have a separate room for functions, don't they?'

'Yes, that's it, but how come you know so much about it?'

'I've a friend, Pru, who works there part-time, between productions, to help make ends meet; and you can spare me the routine about acting and "proper" jobs.'

'I wasn't going to say a word,' said Steve, being somewhat pre-empted.

'That reminds me.' said Jessica, 'I've been meaning to phone her for ages, I must give her a ring later.'

* * *

Saturday arrived, and, as they were dressing to go out, Steve remarked on his wife's apparent good mood.

'Yes,' she replied, 'I'm quite looking forward to this evening in one-way and another.'

They arrived in good time, and enjoyed the usual aperitifs and small talk before taking their places at the table; Jessica sitting opposite Steve.

The food was excellent; everybody appeared to be relishing the convivial atmosphere, albeit in a ceremonious manner. Jessica contemplated the difference in her husband's demeanour compared to his usual behaviour. She wondered whether his fellow Rotarians were aware of the existence of his alter ego.

Directly after the cheese and biscuits, the president rose to his feet and began to make his speech. Jessica wasn't listening, she was trying to catch the eye of the waitress as she moved along the table, refilling glasses.

When she reached Steve, the waitress asked in hushed tones, if he would like his glass topping up. He intimated that he did and reverted his attention, once more, to the speaker. As the waitress slowly refilled Steve's glass, she looked across the table and winked at Jessica.

Suddenly, the waitress jerked bolt upright, her hand clasping her bottom. 'How dare you!' she cried, in a loud voice, and promptly slapped him across the face.

The President stopped speaking; everybody turned to

focus on Steve, giving him disapproving looks.

'I— I—' spluttered Steve, not knowing what to say or do.

With his mouth open and eyebrows raised, he looked frantically up and down the table, full of bewilderment and disbelief. In desperation, he turned to face Jessica, who coolly stared him straight in the eye, and with a sweet, self-satisfied smile, she raised her glass to him.

A Matter of Honour

'It would seem, Mr. Parnham, that you were correct in your assumption that your wife is having an affair.'

'I knew it! That's why I hired you, Blaketon, to be sure. Who is he?

'That is something I haven't yet been able to ascertain, I'm afraid. I've been concentrating my surveillance on your wife. Both parties appear to come and go at an apartment on Highgate Rise, but they never arrive or leave together. Careful not to arouse any suspicion that something is going on.'

'So, that's obviously where the guy lives. It should be easy enough to find out who he is.'

'Er, that's what I thought. I checked Land Registry to see who owns the property and it turns out it is owned by Nookie Holdings.'

'Nookie Holdings? I've never heard of them. It must be

lover boy's company.'

'Again, that's what I thought, so I subsequently made another check and, apparently, the company is owned by a Mrs Louise Parnham.'

'What? My wife? You're telling me this Nookie Holdings is owned by my wife?'

'Yes, sir.'

'But that's not possible: I know nothing about it. Nookie Holdings? It must be her little joke. Well, I've had enough of her shenanigans, she's gone too far this time. I'll put a stop to her getting any more nookie, once and for all.'

'What are you planning Mr Parnham, would you like me to find out who the man is?'

'No, that won't be necessary, thank you. I can handle it from here on in. Just send your bill to me here at Parnham Construction Company and mark it private and confidential – addressee only. That way, it will reach me without anyone else setting eyes on it.'

'As you wish, Mr Parnham.'

And the line went dead.

Jasper Parnham leaned back into his leather chair as he contemplated his next move. It demanded drastic action; for too long, Louise had had free reign to do as she pleased, and this wasn't the first time, by any means, she'd had an affair. Divorce was out of the question; she would want half of the multi- million- pound empire he had built up over the past twenty-eight years. He was not about to relinquish the rewards of all the hard work he'd put into making a success of his business. No, there had to be another solution.

'And what have you busied yourself with today?'

'Oh, the usual, you know. Gym this morning, lunch with the girls and then shopping with Emma this afternoon,' said Louise.

'I really don't know how you manage to fit it all in to your hectic schedule,' said Jasper. 'It must be an absolute godsend having a housekeeper to take care of the day-to-day chores.'

'I never know whether you're being serious or sarcastic.'

'And I never know whether you are taking our union seriously.'

'Our union? That's a strange expression.'

'I mean, our marriage; our relationship; the way we work together; the way we socialise. I sometimes get the impression you're not fully committed. You appear to live a separate life.'

'Well, if you didn't spend so much time working, maybe things would be different.'

'They would be different. For a start, you wouldn't be living in this eight-bedroom house set in fifteen acres. And you wouldn't be driving around in a Mercedes. Also, you might have had to work; heaven forbid.'

'I have my own money.'

'You have the money your parents left you. You didn't have to work for it, like I did.'

'Like *we* did,' blazed Louise. 'I pulled my weight when we started the business. We built it up together, and don't you forget it. So, half of it is mine, anyway. And remember, I know about the shady deals, as well.'

Jasper fell silent. She had just confirmed what he had long-known: she wouldn't go quietly and amicably.

'I thought that would shut you up,' she said. 'You don't like it when someone gets the better of you.'

'We'll see about that. Just you remember, he who laughs last, laughs the loudest.' With that, he stormed off and went to sit on a recliner beside the pool.

Jasper punched a number into his mobile and waited.

'Hello?'

'Hello, Sean, it's Jasper.'

'My god, are you still alive?'

'Yes, I know it's been a long time.'

'I take it you need my assistance with another of your money-making schemes?'

'No, but I'm hoping you can put me in touch with someone who can,' said Jasper.

'Okay, would you care to tell me what it is you need help with? Then I'll know who to ask.'

'I know you have a lot of contacts, so, I was wondering

if you could put me in touch with a hitman?'

'A hitman? My god, are you serious? What— no, I'm not going to ask. It's best I don't know.'

'Yes, I'm serious.'

'Well, I might be able to find out, but it will be a case of knowing a man who knows a man, if you get my drift?

'Yes, okay, I understand. You can give them my mobile number, but under no circumstances are you to reveal my identity; can we be clear about that?'

'Yeah, understood, Jasper. You know you can trust me.'

* * *

The following afternoon, Louise let herself into her apartment on Highgate Rise to find Nick was already there. His tousled, sandy hair added to his good looks. The brightness of his stunning blue eyes told her he was pleased to see her.

'Hello, lover boy. How long have you been here? It's good to know you're still keen.'

'Of course, I'm keen. You're a very sexy and attractive woman: who wouldn't be?'

'You missed out intelligent and rich,' she said.

'Yes, of course. I knew there were other, more important, reasons. So, how are you? When we spoke last night, you seemed to have something troubling you.'

'Oh, it was nothing really. Jasper and I exchanged words, it's nothing new. He doesn't appreciate what he's got in me, and sometimes I have to remind him.'

'Why don't you leave him, then?'

'Because I have a lot of time and money invested in him. If I was to walk out, he would do his damnedest to see I didn't get what is rightfully mine. He's no fool, and he knows a lot of people who can help him get what he wants, or, rather, stop me from getting what I want. I just have to bide my time for now.'

'But I thought you were financially independent of him.'

'I would survive, but only in a straitened manner. Compared to what Jasper and I have together, what I have is a pittance, and I'm not prepared to throw it all away. I want to maintain the lifestyle I've become accustomed to.'

'Doesn't happiness and contentment count for anything?'

'Yes, but only in the right place – like the Seychelles.'

'Money really is important to you, isn't it?'

'It is to most people. Even you need a certain amount of money to live the life you want to live,' said Louise. 'You need to maximise your income - remember that.'

'You said, you were biding your time for now. What did you mean?'

'I meant, until such time I don't have to worry about

money. Like, for instance, Jasper dropping down dead from a heart attack or something; and you never know, you might come into money. Either way, it would mean we could be together. I know that must sound a bit mercenary, but I'm just being practical. I am a woman with needs.'

'I can help to satisfy one of them, if you would care to step into your boudoir.'

* * *

Jasper had just got into his Bentley, to return to his office, when his mobile rang. He looked to see who was calling but the screen said "private number".

'Hello?' he said, tentatively.

'I'm given to understand you've got a job you want doing.'

Job? he thought, momentarily racking his brain before the penny dropped.

'Er, yes. Are you able to do it?'

'Depends what you want doing.'

'I thought you'd been told.'

'I don't know if what I heard was correct. It came from a friend of a friend of a friend. It could have gotten lost in the translation. You know what Chinese whispers are like. You need to tell me what you want doing.'

'Well, I want a termination carried out.'

'In that case, you need a gynaecologist. That's not my field of expertise.'

'No. I mean, as in extermination.'

'Why can't you tell me in plain English what it is you want me to do?'

'I…um, I want you to carry out a hit on someone.'

'We're getting warmer. What kind of hit?'

'Look, have I got to spell it out?'

'Yes, then we would both be on the same page.'

'Okay. Okay. I want someone killed. Is that something you could do?'

'Maybe.'

'Maybe?'

'Depends on who, when, where and how.'

'Right, okay. The who is a Mrs Louise Parnham. The when is as soon as you're able. The where is wherever you think is safest. As for how, I leave that to you. I don't mind how you do it, as long as you do it properly.'

'I'll need some details from you, like where she lives; what she looks like; what her daily routine is; where she works; what car she drives.'

'Okay. She lives in a large, secluded, country house called "Treetops" which is situated about three miles from Saxthorpe on the B2475. She's fifty-one years old, five feet six tall and has shoulder-length chestnut hair. She drives a silver Mercedes SLK, registration 3LP, so, that will be hard to miss. As for her daily routine, there's a lot of uncertainty about that, I'm afraid; but she doesn't work.'

'Okay. I'm going to have to follow her for a while so I can get some idea of her routine. Then I'll know when and where to carry out the job. So, it could take a little while to come to fruition.'

'Understood. Er…How much is…'

'Twenty-grand, up front.'

'But you could take my money and not carry it out, for all I know. How about ten grand up front and the balance on completion?'

'You could pay the ten grand up front and then not pay me the balance, for all I know. It's twenty grand up front – take it or leave it.'

'Okay, you win.'

'Have you got that kind of money?'

'Yes, I'm good for it. How do I pay you?'

'It needs to be in readies, obviously. Put it in a carrier bag and take it to the Ardan Cemetery. Do you know it?'

'Yes.'

'Good. You need to take the path to the right when you enter. About a hundred yards along, you'll see a large, stone archangel on a grave to the right. Three rows back from that, you'll see a grave for Jeremiah Elijah Melville, put the money behind the headstone and then leave. Can you readily access that amount of cash?'

'Yes, It's not a problem.'

'Okay. Place the money behind the headstone at four o'clock tomorrow afternoon, and don't hang about – got it?'

'Got it.'

The deal was done.

Over dinner that evening, Louise said, 'Have you given any thought to what I said the other day?'

'Er…'

'You know, about cutting down on the hours you work?'

'You'd be surprised by what I'm planning to overcome the problem.'

'Oh, good. For once you've actually taken notice of something I've said.'

'Yes, I've finally realised things can't continue the way they have been – I see that now.'

Louise thought how strange it was that Jasper had apparently conceded to her. Maybe this was the opening of a new chapter in their lives. But it also signalled a possible curtailment of her day-to-day activities – and that would never do.

'So, have you decided how it's going to work? Are you going to have set days off each week?' she said.

'Nothing is finalised as yet, but, rest assured, I have set the wheels in motion.'

'So, you are serious about it, then?'

'Oh, yes, deadly serious.'

* * *

'What have you got on for today?' asked Louise, at breakfast. 'Only, I thought, if you took the day off, we could perhaps do something.'

'Sorry, but it's too short notice. I've got a pretty full day ahead of me, and I've got to find time to put some flowers on mother's grave at some point.'

'Oh, yes, I was forgetting it's her birthday. Look, if it will help, I could do that for you.'

'No, no. I have to do it; after all, she was my mother, but thank you for offering. Anyway, I thought you would have had your day all planned.'

'Nothing I couldn't have cancelled or postponed.'

'Let's plan to do something another time,' said Jasper, 'when I can take the day off.'

'Yes, okay. Let me know which day and, in the meantime, I'll try and come up with a few ideas.'

'Sounds like a plan. Right, I best be off if I'm to fit everything in today.'

Jasper was rather buoyant as he got into his car. He was determined to make the most of the time he had left in which he had to put up with his wife. Why not make it as enjoyable as possible? After all, it uses less energy. And the pretence would be bearable knowing he wouldn't have to do it for long. It would also bring a certain *frisson* to his enjoyment.

It was three o'clock when Jasper's secretary brought him a cup of coffee. As she was going out of the door, he said, 'Oh, Penny, I shall be going out shortly and I won't be coming back again today. If anything crops up, pass it over to Jack Litsom; failing that, you can always call me.'

'Yes, of course, Mr Parnham. Thank you.'

Jasper drank his coffee, then picked up his briefcase, opened it and checked again the money was all there before he left the office. On his way to the cemetery, he stopped to pick up some flowers for his mother's grave, arriving at the cemetery just before three forty-five. He transferred the money from the briefcase to a shopping bag, then got out of the car and looked around. Not that he expected to see the man, though he knew he would be under surveillance. He thought it best to go to his mother's grave first, as the man had said not to hang around after he had dropped off the money.

His mother's grave was in the newer part of the cemetery, where a few people could be seen attending to graves. Jasper spent a few minutes tidying the grave before placing the flowers in position and then heading in the opposite direction to drop off the money.

As he walked through the old part, there were fewer people, mainly, he thought, because it dated back to the 18th and 19th centuries. There were several rather impressive monuments erected to denote the resting places of the great and the good; in stark contrast to the unimaginative uniformity of the modern part of the cemetery. Amongst these large edifices, were some trees, which all went towards creating a lot of places for someone to hide from view.

Jasper could see the archangel up a head as he walked along the path. He looked all around trying to catch sight of the man, but there was no sign. He went down beside the archangel until he came to the grave of the nominated, Jeremiah Elijah Melville, 1795 – 1847, which was just about readable. Jasper stood silently and looked around once again. Total silence. Nothing moved. Not even a suggestion of someone lurking in the shadows. He looked at his watch: just gone four. The man must be close by, watching. With a shrug of his shoulders, Jasper put the money behind the headstone and made his way back to the carpark. His part in the conspiracy completed.

* * *

'So, what was it that made you too busy to see me for the past few days?' said Louise.

'I told you, it was just work,' replied Nick. 'Some of us have to do it for a living; and it was you who told me I have to maximise my income, and that's exactly what I was doing. I had told the man I would do it, and I'm a man of my word.'

'But four days to knock up an aviary for a few birds?'

'It was four pens for one thousand pheasants.'

'What, so they can be safely reared before being released so you lot can shoot them?'

'What lot?'

'The hunting, shooting and fishing brigade.'

'It's the way of the countryside, and I've never known you to pass on the opportunity of having roast pheasant on your plate.'

'Yes, well… Talking of food, how about we go to a country pub and get some lunch, rather than stay in here? It's such a lovely day.'

'I'd like that,' said Nick. 'How about "The Highwayman"? We've been there a few times, and the food is good.'

'Okay.'

'Right, well we hadn't better leave together: I'll go first and get a table and you can follow on in ten minutes.'

'Okay, off you go, I'll see you in a bit.'

Jasper was rather unsettled sitting at his desk. He felt a bit jittery – on edge. He had no idea when the hitman would strike, and every time the phone rang he would grab it, thinking it was the police. But then, if it had happened, they would find him and tell him in person, he reasoned. In reality, the hitman was probably still following her to get an idea of her movements, and then he would have to plan the hit. So, yes, it was still early days, and it all comes to he who waits.

'Oh, you're here,' said Jasper, as he walked in through the door that evening.

'Of course, I am,' said Louise. 'Where did you think I'd be?'

'I…er, I don't know. I suppose I thought you might be er…still out with your friends doing something or other.'

'Oh, no. I always make a point of being here for when you get back, so I can pander to your every need,' she said, sarcastically.

'Huh, chance would be a fine thing. I'm going to shower and get changed before dinner.'

As he walked away, Louise's phone rang. She looked at the screen which said "private number".

'Hello?'

'Is that Mrs Louise Parnham?'

'I'm sorry, I can't hear you clearly. Who is it?'

'It doesn't matter who I am.'

'I can't hear you: you're very muffled.'

'Is that any better?'

'A bit. Who are you, and what do you want?'

'I have some information for you.'

'You have an inflammation?'

'No. I have some information for you.'

'About what? Who are you?'

'Look, just listen carefully, lady. Your husband has hired me to kill you.'

'Is this some kind of joke?'

'No. I'm deadly serious. He's paid me twenty-grand to do it.'

Louise suddenly felt like she'd been hit in the solar plexus: it had taken her breath away. She was floundering, trying to come to terms with the enormity of what the man had just said. She began to shake and sat down, feeling weak at the knees. Her husband had hired someone to kill her. Was this really happening? But there was something in the man's muffled voice which told her he was for real.

'W—Why are you telling me this?' Louise found herself saying.

'Because I wondered if you would like to make a counter offer?'

'A counter offer? What do you mean?'

'It's quite simple. For twenty-five grand I would kill your husband instead.'

'But that's—' Louise broke off from what she was about to say, as a moment of clarity appeared from the myriad of thoughts and emotions coursing through her. This could be the answer. She would have the house, the business and all the money for a mere twenty-five grand. It was a no-brainer. 'That's a splendid idea,' she continued.

'So, you'd like to go ahead, would you?'

'I'm sorry?'

'You want me to do it, then?'

'Yes, yes.'

'Can you get hold of that amount in readies?'

'It will take me a couple of days, but, yes, I can.'

'Good. So, on Thursday, take the money, in a carrier bag, to Ardan Cemetery. Turn right and follow the path for about a hundred yards and you'll see a large archangel on the right. Three rows back from that, you'll see a grave for Jeremiah Elijah Melville, put the money behind the headstone and leave.'

'Okay, what time?'

'Make it four o'clock.'

'Okay. Er…how will you do it?'

'You don't need to worry your pretty little head about that.'

And the line went dead.

* * *

'Hello, Nick, it's me, Louise.'

'I knew that. These modern phones tell you who's calling before you answer. You should get one.'

'Very funny. Listen, I need to talk to you about a phone call I received last night.'

'Oh, okay, go ahead.'

'No, not now, on the phone. Can I meet you at the apartment?'

'Er…yes. I'm free this afternoon, say two o'clock-ish?'

'Yes, that's fine with me. Sorry, I've got to go. See you later. Bye.'

Then doubt began to creep in. Would she be doing the right thing in telling him? The less people who knew, the better, she reasoned. After all, she would go to prison if it came to light she had paid someone to murder Jasper. And Nick would be incriminated if he had known about it and not reported it. But she desperately needed to talk it through with someone. It was too much of a burden for her to bear on her own. To pay someone to murder her husband, was one hell of a gamble to take but the rewards would be immense.

Jasper was having a full-on day at work and wished he was anywhere other than there. He remembered what Louise had said about taking a day off and doing something together. Was there any point? he asked himself. She was due to be bumped off any time soon. It didn't matter, he needed to have a break and there was no reason why he couldn't make her remaining days pleasurable, if only for old time's sake.

He picked up the phone to speak to his secretary. 'Penny, could you bring in my diary, please?'

'Yes, Mr Parnham.'

Ten seconds later she entered his office. 'How's it looking for next week?'

'Well, you've got appointments throughout the week,' she said.

'Here, let me have a look. Umm…oh dear. No. Look. I'm going to take the Wednesday off. Ring Palmer and Bagget and reschedule the appointments for another day.'

'Yes, Mr Parnham. Of course.' And with that, she went back to her desk to make the calls, leaving Jasper to contemplate the possible vagaries of a day with Louise.

Louise sat in the apartment mulling over the situation she found herself in, while she waited for Nick. She was still undecided about whether or not she should tell him. But there was no doubting how much it was weighing her down. She knew the benefits of talking over a problem with someone; however, this was way beyond a normal problem. There were high stakes involved; they couldn't be any higher.

She went to the kitchen to make a cup of coffee just as Nick arrived.

'You must have smelt the coffee,' she called out.

'My timing is nothing short of perfection,' he said.

Nick sat down just as Louise brought the drinks through. 'So, what's this mysterious phone call about that you couldn't discuss on the phone?'

'And how are you today, Louise?' she said.

'I'm sorry. Yes. How are you?'

'That's better. If I said, fine, I would be lying.'

'I take it it's that phone call which is responsible for how you're feeling.'

'Yes.'

'Would you care to tell me about it? Maybe I can help.'

'If I were to tell you, you couldn't help me, anyway.'

'Are you sure?'

'I'm positive; and it wouldn't be fair on you if I did.'

'How come?'

'I would be putting you in an invidious position. You would probably be compromised.'

'Let me worry about that. It's obviously something serious; you'd feel better for getting it off your chest.'

'I know I would, but…'

'Look, I will stand by you no matter what, and, if I can't help, then you could count on my full support.'

'That's very sweet of you but you have no idea of the implications, should I tell you.'

'How bad can it be?'

'If I were to tell you, I would be intrusting you with my life.'

'Seriously?'

'Seriously.'

'Oh my god, Lou, what have you got yourself into?'

'It wasn't my doing: it was forced upon me. Last night

I received a call from this man who claimed Jasper had paid him twenty grand to kill me.'

'What? Why would your husband want you dead when all he had to do was divorce you?'

'For the same reasons I wouldn't divorce him: he wants to hold onto everything; the house, the business and the money. We haven't seen eye to eye on anything for years. And the fact, I know everything about his secrets and dodgy dealings is reason enough for not divorcing me. So, I suppose, he saw this as the only way to overcome all the inherent problems.'

'But why on earth would this hitman tell you what he was going to do?'

'Because he was after more money.'

'But why tell you? Surely, he would go back to your husband if that's the case.'

'No. He is cleverer than that. He said if I were to pay him twenty-five-grand he would kill my husband instead.'

'What did you say?'

'Eventually, I agreed. I had no choice. Had I told him to get lost, he would have just gone ahead and killed me, anyway. So, by paying him the money I get to live. It was Hobson's Choice: Jasper or me. Either way he is going to kill one of us.'

'And get forty-five grand for doing it,' said Nick. 'Very astute.'

'That's not the word I would've used.'

'So, have you paid him yet?'

'No. I've got to put the money behind a headstone in Ardan Cemetery tomorrow afternoon.'

'I can't let you do that: I'll take the money and drop it off.'

'No, no. I can't risk that. He'll be watching and if he sees you there, it could put the whole operation in jeopardy. I can't afford to take that chance.'

'Well, I never would have guessed in a hundred years that would be your problem. It's like something you read in a novel or watch on television.'

'If this goes according to plan, I will have gained my freedom and financial security. And after a respectful length of time there's no reason why we couldn't be together.'

'Every cloud…'

'Hello. Had a good day?' enquired Louise, as Jasper walked in the door.

'No. It was hell. I just want to forget about it.'

'Oh, sorry to hear that,' she said, as if she cared.

'But it did make me do something.'

'Oh, yes?'

'Yes. I've booked a day off for Wednesday of next week. So, have you anything in mind apropos what you'd like to do?'

Well, I have an idea that I'll need to firm up before I

tell you. Something calm and peaceful will be the order of the day. It will be so relaxing: just what you need.'

'Steady on, old girl. You had me going there for a moment.'

'Well, let yourself go. I am being sincere for once. It really will be calm, peaceful and relaxing.'

'What are you up to?'

'Nothing. I just thought it would make a change if we did something nice for once. A trip down memory lane, if you like, to happier times.'

'Okay, what have you done?'

'I haven't done anything. I just want to cease hostilities for a day. Is there anything wrong with that?'

'Umm…I suppose not,' he said begrudgingly.

* * *

It was nearly ten o'clock on a bright Thursday morning when Louise pulled into the carpark of Beauchamps Health Club and Spa, where she had arranged to meet her friend, Diane, for a few treatments and a bit of pampering. It still troubled her that Jasper had actually paid someone to kill her: it felt quite surreal. It didn't happen in the real world, did it? But, as she had found out, it obviously did. And she, too, was now playing an active part in the dark portals of the underworld. However, had it come to this? In a strange sort of way, she felt one step removed from it as she wouldn't be the one dirtying her hands, and she wouldn't have to witness it either. That should help when it came to dealing with the aftermath.

Feeling suitably refreshed and with their skin aglow, Louise and Diane headed for a buffet lunch and a glass of bubbly in the dining room.

'Is something troubling you?' said Diane. 'You seem to have something on your mind; you're not your normal self.'

'Oh, it's nothing really, just life, I guess.'

'We've known each other for more years than I care to remember, you would tell me if something was wrong, wouldn't you?'

'Yes. Yes, of course I would,' said Louise. 'Take no notice of me, everything is fine.' Hoping she sounded more convincing than she felt.

'You can call me anytime; you know that, don't you?'

'Thank you.'

'So, what have you got planned for this afternoon?'

'I've got to go into the city. I have some business to attend to at the bank.'

'Would you like me to come with you?'

'No, I'll be fine. There's no need for you to worry about me, I'm a big girl now,' said Louise, with a smile.

After Louise had collected the money and safely

deposited it behind the headstone, she breathed a lot easier. She was now safe from an untimely death. The euphoria she now felt had lifted the weight from her shoulders. The gentle summer's breeze of the late afternoon danced upon her senses – she felt alive once more.

As Louise pulled up in front of her house, her phone rang. It was Nick.

'Hello?'

'Hello, Lou. How did it go? Were there any problems? Did anything happen?'

'No. Everything went like clockwork. I didn't see anyone and I wasn't followed. I told you there wouldn't be any problems. It's a great feeling getting my life back.'

'I can imagine.'

'I don't suppose it will be too long before Jasper starts wondering why I'm still alive.'

'And vice versa.'

'Yes, it will be awful waiting and not knowing when it will happen. I'm not so sure I'll be able to cope with the suspense. It will only get worse the longer it goes on.'

'I'll always be here to talk to, you know that.'

'Yes. I wasn't all that keen to tell you about it, but it did help, so I'm glad I did. Thank you.'

'No problem, it's what I'm here for.'

* * *

'Are you in a position, yet, to tell me what my fate is to be on Wednesday?'

'You make it sound like I'm a judge about to pass sentence on you for some heinous deed,' said Louise.

'That's just about the measure of it,' Jasper said, putting his knife and fork down on an empty plate.

'But you were all for having a day out together. Have you changed your mind?'

'Not necessarily. It depends what you've got lined up.'

'Okay. Well, Geoff and Marcia have agreed to let us borrow their boat for the day.'

'Really?'

'Yes, really.'

'Well, that's different. It's been such a long time since we were on the Norfolk Broads. For once, you've managed to get something right.'

'Coming from you, I'll take that as a compliment.'

'God. Had I known, I wouldn't have said it. I must be going soft in my old age.'

'His new boat is fully equipped for life on board. In fact, it would be possible to live on it.'

'Well, don't go getting any fanciful ideas: we're going for a day trip down the River Bure – that's all.'

'Aye, aye, capt'n.'

'Oh, please!'

'Oh, come on, Jasper, lighten up. We're going to have a nice day away from it all. At least try and enter into the spirit of things.'

'I'm going, aren't I?'

'I suppose, for you, that passes as being in the spirit. Before long you'll actually smile when you talk about it, if you're not careful.'

'And it's sarky comments like that which will put paid to it, if *you're* not careful.'

'Oh, I give up. I don't know why I bother. I'm off to find someone more agreeable to talk to.' And with that, Louise got up, grabbed her handbag and walked out to her car.

'So, tell me what happened,' said Nick, as they sat in the apartment. 'What made you walk out?'

'That bloody man. The sooner the hitman does his job, the better. I got him to agree to taking a day off on Wednesday. I arranged everything so we could have a boat on the Broads for a day to get away from it all. But he's as enthusiastic as a turkey in the run up to Christmas. I thought it would do us both good.'

'So, what are you going to do?'

'I imagine we'll probably still go. We're borrowing the boat from friends of ours, and I don't particularly want to tell them we've had an argument and no longer want the boat.'

'If you're arguing or not speaking, that boat is going to seem awfully small.'

'It's forty-two feet long. There's enough space to keep our distance.'

'In that case, it will seem like a very long day.'

'Yes, I know. I'm hoping that once we are sailing down the Bure, he will enjoy it and there'll be a personality transformation.'

'More like a miracle, if you ask me.'

'Not necessarily. He – we – used to enjoy boating back in the day, so, if this doesn't work, then nothing will. But then, having said that, it doesn't really matter, does it? He's going to die soon, anyway. So why am I even bothering? It doesn't make any sense.'

'Maybe you have a sub-conscience desire to rekindle the love you once had for each other.'

'I've just paid out twenty-five grand to have him killed, so I don't think that's the case, do you?'

'Stranger things have happened.'

'Well, as far as I know, there's no blue moon in the offing.'

'So, where are you setting off from? Where's the boat moored?'

'Wroxham.'

'Oh, I see. It gets a bit busy around there.'

'Yes, but everything moves slowly on the water. You know, I was so looking forward to this day out but Jasper's attitude has put a damper on it. I never should have bothered.'

'I suppose, you've just got to tell yourself, very soon it will all be over, then you can begin to enjoy life once more.'

'Yes, you're right. "Always look on the bright side of life", as the song goes.'

* * *

'Come on, Jasper, get a move on. I've packed a picnic hamper as I'm not going to waste time cooking on board the boat and I've no desire to go to some busy riverside pub to eat, either. The idea is to get away from people.'

'Yes, okay. I'm just getting my things together.'

'No,' said Louise, looking across at him. 'We are not taking phones and laptops with us. We do not want any contact with the outside world today.'

'But what about in the case of an emergency?'

'There isn't going to be one. What do you think people did before the advent of mobile phones?'

'Something might come up at work which needs my attention.'

'It won't be anything that can't keep for a day. Anyway, what do you employ managers for, if not to deal with problems as they arise? Now, come on, we're meeting Geoff and Marcia at the marina at nine o'clock. Let's get moving.'

'How lovely to see you both,' said Marcia, as Louise and Jasper boarded the boat.

'Welcome aboard the "Little Escape", said Geoff.

'How appropriate a name is that for our day out,' said Louise.

'You've certainly got a glorious day for it,' continued Geoff. 'I've lowered the canopy for you, and I'll just run through everything with you, Jasper, so you know how it all works.'

'And while they're doing that, Louise, I'll show you what's what on the rest of the boat,' said Marcia.

Once Louise and Jasper were happy with everything, Geoff and Marcia wished them *"bon voyage"* as they slipped the mooring ropes and cautiously eased the boat out into the river.

It was happening.

Louise stood on the raised cockpit of the boat beside Jasper, who was steering the boat with a look of concentration on his face.

'Everything okay?' she enquired.

'Yes, yes. It will take me a little while to get the feel of her, but nothing I can't manage.'

'Okay. Good. I'm just going to put the food in the fridge along with the champagne. Fancy a cup of tea?'

'Yes, why not? I'm glad this isn't going to be a dry ship.'

Louise thought she detected a subtle thawing in his

demeanour. Nothing to overt, but, nonetheless, she thought there might be a glimmering – a soupçon. Cause for optimism.

Louise sat in the navigator's seat drinking in the beauty of Nature as they sailed along at a steady four miles-an-hour. This was the life, sun shining, a slight breeze riffling through your hair. There was an abundance of wildlife, and neither sight nor sound of any motor vehicles – sheer bliss. She looked across at Jasper, who was wearing a relaxed expression on his face. Something she hadn't seen in a long time. It seemed like he was at last free of the burdens in life which weighed him down.

'What? What are you looking at me like that for?'

'I'm seeing a different you,' she replied.

'A different me, whatever are you talking about?'

'You're relaxed for once and it shows in your face. You're now rediscovering how good life can be if only you'd let it.'

Jasper gave some thought to what she had said before saying, 'I think there may be an element of truth in what you said, though it pains me to admit it.'

'You've spent the last – god knows how many – years working, working and working. That's all your life has consisted of. Is it any wonder we drifted apart? Yes, we have a beautiful house and cars, but what's the point in being able to have the finer things in life if you don't take the time to enjoy them.'

'There'll be time enough when I retire.'

'Retire? The way you're going, you won't live long enough to. You're overweight, you have a stressful job and you don't exercise. You're a prime candidate for a heart-attack.'

Jasper sat in silence as he mulled over what Louise had said. He knew she was right, but he'd never stopped to give it any consideration. He'd never had the time to give it due diligence. He knew of people who had been forced to take stock of and radically change their lifestyle as a result of a health scare or some other major event. The thing is, he'd always thought it was something which only happened to other people and not him. Maybe now was the right time to address the matter.

'Okay, I hear what you're saying and I realise it is something which I need to give some serious thought to.'

'You will do it, though, won't you, give it some thought?'

'Yes.'

My god, thought Louise, maybe there will be a blue moon tonight after all. Maybe this boat trip will reap more dividends than I ever dared hope for.

'Are you feeling peckish yet?' she asked. 'If so, you need to pull in somewhere and we can have our picnic.'

'Okay. It looks as if there are some moorings a bit further up; I'll pull in there.'

'Aye, aye, skipper. I'll stand by ready with the rope.'

'Be careful, I know of someone who jumped ashore to moor up the boat and slipped, smashing his hip and pelvis. He never did fully recover.'

'Do I look that stupid?'

'I'm just saying be careful, that's all.'

'I'm touched that you care.'

'Yeah, well…'

Over a leisurely seafood platter and bottle of bubbly, they continued talking. Louise couldn't remember the last time they'd had such a meaningful conversation. It was like she was talking to a different person. Jasper had never been so loquacious.

'Fancy another glass? I think we can squeeze another glass each out of the bottle,' said Louise.

'Why not? It's turning out to be a better day than I had anticipated.'

'Good. I'm really pleased you're enjoying it.'

'It's quite amazing how a day on the river, with good food and champagne, can make you so relaxed. It has shown me there is more to life than work, and that is down to you.'

'All I did was arrange things and make the odd observation, you did the rest.'

'You should have done this a long time ago. You've made me see the error of my ways. There is more to life than work, I can see that now. But it has come at a price and too late, I fear.'

'What do you mean?'

'I can see now how I drove you into the arms of other men. I was so wrapped up in my work, I didn't give you the attention you needed – you deserved. And it's probably only a matter of time before you walk out on me, and that's what I deserve. I couldn't realistically expect you to do any different. But I've done something which…'

'Which?'

'Which…I can stop. At least I hope I can. That's supposing you see things the same way as me.'

'Jasper, you're talking in riddles. What are you trying to say?'

'I guess it's to do with today. We've been like a normal married couple. We've been having normal conversations – interactions – and it has reminded me of how it used to be and what I've been missing. I know I've done some awful things in my time but maybe this is my coming of age. The time when I've finally seen the wood in the trees. All the time it was there right under my nose but I never saw it. How stupid was I?'

'Well, I suppose I've also been guilty of doing some stupid things in my time. Though, in my defence, I would say I was driven to it. I had everything I desired but nobody to share it with. I had too much time on my hands which inevitably led to some indiscretions. In fact, I would go so far as to say, I grew to resent you. You gave me whatever I wanted just to keep me out of your hair. You thought I was happy as long as you kept giving me expensive jewellery or a new car. Over the years I developed a life independent of you. I had my own circle of friends which kept me occupied during the day. But you were never interested in what I had been doing. We were like the proverbial ships passing in the night – I hated it.'

'Is it too late, do you think, to salvage something from the wreckage?'

'That would largely depend on you,' said Louise. 'How serious you are about changing your life, and not going back to your old ways once this day is over.'

'I can only prove that to you if you give me a chance. Today has been a kind of epiphany for me. I realise what's important in life, albeit belatedly. But if we can work together, I believe there are sufficient grounds to give us hope for the future. And I am fully committed to working towards that.'

Louise looked into his eyes as she processed all that he'd said. She saw a radiant sparkle full of hope reflected. There was a burning desire – a passion - within those bright, brown orbs, which told her he was sincere.

'Okay, I believe you, and I think we can move forward. Without trying to be overly sanguine, this could be the first day of the rest of our lives. Cheers,' said Louise, raising her glass.

'To the future,' responded Jasper.

'How much further can we go? We have to allow enough time to get back,' said Louise.

'Good point. I was hoping to make it to Hickling Broad and the nature reserve, but we're not going to have enough time for that. On the map, it shows an inlet a bit further on, there should be enough water there to enable us to turn around safely.'

'Well, it's been a lovely day,' said Louise, as they headed back along the River Bure to Wroxham. 'Who would have thought it would turn out the way it has?'

'Are you able to tie up any "loose ends", so to speak, to make this fresh start?'

'That's very diplomatic of you, but, yes, there are a couple of matters I need to attend to. One, of which, might prove difficult.'

'Oh, dear. How come? Can I help in any way?'

'Well, theoretically, you may actually be able to, I think.'

'Good. How so?'

'There's an elephant in the boat. Something we've both failed to mention.'

Jasper looked puzzled. 'I don't understand.'

'I think you do. There is something you arranged to

happen, isn't there?'

Oh, that. Yes. I... er, um...How do you know about it?'

'The hitman told me, and offered to take you out instead for more money, so I paid him. It was either you or me; either way, one of us was going to die.'

'God, what are we going to do? He could strike at any moment.'

'Well,' said Louise. 'I have no way of contacting him to cancel the order. You, on the other hand, must be able to make contact because you instigated it in the first place.'

'Oh, yes. Brilliant! But I can't do it right now because we left our phones behind. Remember?'

'You'll just have t—'

At that very moment, as they entered a bend in the river, there came a loud crack. The unmistakable report from a high-velocity rifle. There was a momentary silence – a hiatus – which seemed to last a long time. Louise knew instinctively what had happened. She looked down to see Jasper slumped on the deck with a bullet hole to his head. She stared at him in a state of suspension. Her brain not registering what her eyes were seeing. She slowly shook her head in disbelief as the message gradually filtered through. Eventually it came. Louise gave vent to heart-rendering scream which scorched her throat. Then the floodgates opened and she sobbed and sobbed.

Time stood still.

When Louise looked up, the boat was heading directly for the bank, where there was a wooded area. She had to step over the body to get to the wheel. She pulled on the wheel as hard and fast as she could to take the boat back to the middle of the river, but to no avail. The boat struck a branch of a tree which was hanging low over the water. The boat ran aground and was listing, which caused Louise to lose her balance and fall overboard and into the shallow edge of the river.

As she struggled to her feet, she heard the sound of footsteps moving quickly through the undergrowth. It came as a relief knowing help was on the way. How on earth was she going to explain what happened to the police?

Louise became aware somebody was watching her. She looked up and was confronted by an athletically built man wearing camouflage clothing. His piercing blue eyes looked out from beneath the peak of a matching, camouflage cap. He was holding a rifle across his chest.

'You! What the f— All along y—' She was shocked by the revelation. Her mind frantically trying to work out how it could possibly have been.

'I expect this must come as something of a surprise,' said Nick.

'You can say that again,' she said, the tears now dissipated. 'How could you deceive and mislead me?'

'Well, think about it. I can't afford to have people knowing what I do, can I?'

'But you took my money.'

'Business is business. As you told me, you have to maximise your income.'

'I thought I was more to you than just a meal ticket.'

'You should know, you don't mix business with pleasure.'

'So where does that leave us now?'

'I still have one more contract to fulfil.'

'You don't mean—'

In a cool and calm manner, Nick smoothly raised the gun and put a single bullet in her forehead.

Prey For Survival

It was another hot, sultry day in the African savannah and Petra, the lioness, and her three young cubs were trying to keep in what little shade was afforded them.

'We're hot and hungry,' whined one of the cubs.

'Patience,' replied Petra. 'Something will come along soon.'

'But it's been over two weeks since we last had anything to eat. Look, you can see all of our ribs.'

It pained their mother to see her cubs visually displaying the effects of the hunger, which was savaging their bodies. Petra had been searching tirelessly for prey – hopefully a zebra or an antelope – but the truth was, the watering holes had all but dried up. And the long wait at this one was also proving to be fruitless.

'Yes, I know. It's affecting me as well, but I'm doing everything I can.'

Looking at her cubs, she wondered how the rest of the pride were doing, as they had gone in different directions in their quest for food.

As the morning progressed, the lioness lay still and ever vigilant. Panting in order to try and regulate her temperature and conserve energy in the unforgiving sun. Suddenly, Petra's ears pricked up and she raised herself up onto all fours. She had detected something over the far side of the watering hole, amongst the scrub. Motionless, she stood staring intently, waiting for a glimpse or sign of whatever was heading towards her.

'Shush!' she hissed at the cubs. 'All of you, be quiet.' Cautiously she took a few paces forward, her eyes peeled, surveying the landscape in anticipation. Her patience started to pay dividends when a small herd of antelope emerged from the scrub heading towards the watering hole.

'Okay, nice and easy does it,' said Petra, quietly to herself, licking her lips in anticipation. Another quick glance behind to check on her cubs, who also stood still as if they knew the importance of the next few minutes. Those minutes seemed like hours as Petra continued to track the progress of the antelope, which were getting ever closer.

The tension was palpable.

There came an almost imperceptible sound from behind them. The three cubs all turned to see what it was.

'What was that?' one of the cubs said, as they started to retreat.

'I don't know,' said Petra, frantically looking in that direction.

Her panting had now stopped and her chest cavity was going in and out as her heart thumped away. She remained motionless, but her head was swivelling back and forth trying to weigh up the situation. Should she go and investigate what was approaching from behind and risk losing the chance of a desperately needed meal? It was a tough call. They needed the food but she also had another intuitive instinct: to protect her cubs should they be in danger.

As time slipped by, the presence of whatever was coming up from the rear, became apparent as it got ever closer. Petra's eyes and ears were working overtime as she tried to discover what it was. Then a glance forward to check the antelope were still approaching.

The cubs were now aware of something getting ever closer from behind and looked searchingly at their mother for reassurance.

'What is it? What is it?'

Petra looked again beyond the cubs and saw a pack of hyenas moving through the scrub. She had a stark choice: chase off the hyenas and scare the antelope, or catch the antelope and lose her cubs. She was caught between the Devil and the deep blue sea. Both were very important to her. She had to think – and fast.

Petra knew the odds of her being able to protect all three cubs from a pack of hyenas were stacked against her. She was only one and they were many. She desperately needed to eat, as did the cubs, and there was no telling when the next opportunity would present itself.

Petra looked beseechingly at her young cubs. What could they possibly know about this quandary she was faced with? They had implicit trust in her to protect them and feed them, they were totally dependent on her for everything. And, sadly, she was going to let them down no matter which decision she made.

Then it happened.

There was a loud report which severed the tense silence of the savannah. Immediately, the antelope sprang into evasive action. They turned as one and bolted back into the scrub in their familiar bouncing gait – an instinctive survival technique. At the same time, the hyenas stopped abruptly in their tracks as their heads turned towards the direction the repercussion had come from. And then, they too, ran off in the opposite direction, to put as much distance as possible between them and this new, unseen danger.

Silence now returned to the savannah once more, save for the crying and whining of the cubs as they stood over their mother's lifeless body, which had a single, fatal gunshot wound to her head.

All That Glitters

It was five o'clock when the stillness of the night was split by the high-pitched shrill of an alarm clock.

'For God's sake turn that damn thing off; it's Sunday.'

Digby did as he was told and apologised to his wife. He laid there for a few minutes to allow himself to wake up. His wife couldn't understand why he had to get up at this unearthly hour on a Sunday. She didn't share his passion; she thought he was barking. But Digby still got a rush of adrenaline when he thought about the prospects of what lay ahead. Today could be the day when his diligence paid off; it had to happen sooner or later. Then his wife would change her tune – oh yes!

He slipped out of bed and went to the bathroom, and, after showering, went downstairs and got himself some breakfast, after which, he set off on his mission. It was something he did on a fairly regular basis at weekends, and his enthusiasm never waned. He was driven by an eternal optimism that today could be the day.

It was just on six-thirty when Digby pulled into the carpark at the front of the community centre. He had timed it perfectly. The car-booters were setting up their stalls in the field behind. Already, there were one or two dealers standing and watching as people unloaded their cars and vans, ready to grab anything remotely valuable from an unsuspecting and unknowing stallholder. Digby wasn't a dealer, but he had learnt he needed to be there at this time if he was to stand any chance of finding a bargain before the crowds arrived.

There were bargains to be had. He had seen people who had taken an item, they'd bought at a car-boot sale for a few pounds, to be valued by an expert on the television; only for it to be subsequently valued at hundreds, if not thousands, of pounds.

Digby was no expert, but he felt he knew enough to be able to recognise a bargain when he saw one. He had picked up a few nice pieces over the years, but nothing of any great value. His wife referred to them as old tat which cluttered up the house. She couldn't see, or appreciate, the beauty in them, or the craftsmanship of the artisans. In her view, why would anybody spend a lot of money on something which was old, when you could go out and buy a new one for a lot less?

She was a philistine.

Digby had to move quickly from stall to stall, but at the same time he had to be thorough in his search. If he was to miss something, there were others who would readily snatch it up. Some of the stallholders would get a bit tetchy when dealers pounced on stuff before they'd had a chance to set out their stall. Digby always made a point of looking in the bottom of boxes; you never knew what you might find.

He was becoming ever-more energized as he moved amongst the various stalls, trying to get there before the vultures descended. There were cars still filtering onto the field, so there would be more opportunities to get first dibs.

Digby was looking through the assortment of antiques and collectables which a man had just dumped on the trestle as he unloaded his car. There wasn't anything which immediately stood out, but as he moved away his foot caught something propped up against the leg of the table. He looked down and saw four or five paintings leaning on top of each other. Flicking through them, he pulled out one for a closer inspection. It was in a style he was familiar with. Could this really be what he thought it was? His heart was pounding and hands shaking as he studied the painting. It wasn't signed but it had to be by John Crome; it was unmistakable. Digby looked around to see if anybody was watching, but no one was paying any attention to him.

Good.

At long last his perseverance had paid off; he had found something which had slipped through the net, and was worth a lot of money. But he had yet to find out how much the man wanted for it. Digby tried to contain his excitement and appear casual so as not to arouse any suspicion that it was something out of the ordinary.

But it was!

He couldn't believe his luck. This was something which always happened to other people.

'Excuse me. How much are you asking for this painting?' said Digby, in a voice he didn't recognise.

The man took the painting and gave it a once-over. 'Original oil on canvas…fifty quid?'

Digby nearly bit his hand off, but still trying to be indifferent, he heard himself say, 'Will you take thirty?'

The man gave it some thought and came back with, 'Forty?'

Digby pursed his lips and shook his head. 'I'll go to thirty-five.' Oh my god, he thought, did I really say that?

'Go on then,' the man said, handing back the painting.

Digby could barely contain himself as he eagerly handed over the money.

Over the past couple of years, Digby had developed a particular interest in paintings, partly due to the influence of his friend, Gerry, who was an avid and knowledgeable collector. He couldn't wait to show him this "John

Crome" which he'd bought for only thirty-five pounds.

Yes. Thirty-five pounds!

He'll be green with envy. All those early mornings had finally paid off. But he wouldn't be looking for an early return on his money because he was going to hang it in pride of place on his wall, irrespective of what his wife, Anne, might have to say.

It was a jubilant Digby who drove home later that morning. He thought he'd offer to take Anne out for Sunday lunch, by way of a small celebration to mark his good fortune.

'Is this your way of easing your conscience for wasting more money on junk?' said Anne, when he asked her if she would like to go out to lunch.

'No. And it's not junk. This painting must be worth at least two grand.'

'Oh yeah? And you bought it for thirty-five? Who are you trying to kid?

'I'm telling you the man didn't know what he had. You wait until Gerry sees it: he'll tell you what it's worth. Now, do you want to go out to lunch or not?'

'Yes,' she said. 'I don't see why I shouldn't benefit from your delusional theories.'

'Look, how about asking Gerry and Lisa if they'd like to come with us? It'll be good to have a catch-up.'

Over drinks, as they waited for their food to arrive, Gerry said, 'So tell me about this painting you acquired.'

'Oh, don't get him started,' said Anne.

'You mean the "John Crome"' Digby replied. 'I picked it up at a car-boot sale this morning.'

'Is it signed?'

'No, but I'm positive it has to be by him. The style is unmistakable; and to think, I only paid thirty-five pounds for it!'

'I look forward to seeing it,' said Gerry.

'You won't have to wait long; I brought it with me to show you; it's in the car.'

Anne turned to Lisa and rolled her eyes. 'More tat for me to dust.'

'It won't be tat if Digby's right about the painting, will it?' replied Lisa.

'You really think he's made a one in a million find that's worth thousands?'

'It does happen.'

'Not to him, it doesn't.'

It was Digby's turn to roll his eyes. 'I'm afraid Anne's taste is very much of a contemporary nature. She would probably turn her nose up at *"The Fighting Temeraire"*.'

'You're the one who has the temerity,' said Anne. 'Bringing all that rubbish home.'

'I said, "*The Temeraire*" not the tem— oh, forget it.'

Digby had long-since accepted that they were never

going to see eye-to-eye over antiques; but his wife did, somewhat, put a damper on his enjoyment. He had often thought how nice it would be to have a house large enough for them to each have a room of their own. Then he could indulge himself to his heart's content, having his antiques and paintings on display and not having to listen to the constant moaning and sniping.

If only.

When the food arrived, the conversation turned to more existential issues, engineered by Anne and Lisa; like what was happening in Coronation Street and EastEnders. Again, Digby rolled his eyes. Why they couldn't watch something interesting like the antiques programmes, he'd never know and couldn't even begin to understand.

But, *c'est la vie.*

After their meal, they walked to their cars and Gerry said, 'Right, let's have a look at this painting, then.'

Digby took it out of the boot of his car. 'What do you think to this little beauty?'

Gerry took the painting from him and studied it closely. 'It's very nice and it is well-executed, and it would appear to be in the style of John Crome. But, as you said, it isn't signed. It looks to me like the scene is of Ludham.'

'Really?' said Digby. 'That's where I grew up. Yes, I can see it is now you've pointed it out.'

Gerry continued to study the painting, saying, 'Yes, it

looks like one of his.' He turned the painting to look at the verso, which could sometimes hold vital information.

'Ah.'

'Ah? What do you mean, ah? What have you found?'

'Well, I don't know how to tell you this.'

'Tell me what?'

'I'm afraid this isn't a John Crome original.'

Digby was dumbfounded. 'W—What? But it has to be. What makes you say that?'

'Look here,' said Gerry, pointing to where the canvas was attached to the stretcher.

'What's wrong with that?'

'The nails attaching the canvas are galvanized. John Crome died in 1821, and I think you'll find that the galvanizing process wasn't invented until sometime later.'

Digby's mouth was hanging open. He was apoplectic.

Anne quickly chimed in, 'See, what did I tell you? Nothing but rubbish. Maybe you'll listen to me in future.'

Suddenly, it felt like the bottom had dropped out of his world. Digby had lost all credibility as far as his wife was concerned. In future, it would be even more difficult to convince her he knew what he was talking about. His confidence had taken a bit of a knock. No more could he be certain about anything when it came to antiques. He thought he had joined the ranks of those who had bought something for a song and subsequently found it to be worth a fortune. It was true, wasn't it? It only happened to other people.

'No. I can't believe it,' said Digby. 'I was so sure. Well, that's it; I don't want the painting anymore.'

'But you liked it when you bought it, and it's still the same painting,' said Gerry.

'Yes, I know. But I thought it was a John Crome original, and what I've got now is a copy – a fake. I don't want it. If you like it, you can have it.'

'Well, okay, if you're sure. But at least let me give you the money, then I would feel free to do what I like with it.'

'Whatever.'

Digby really didn't want to know. He had lost his spark. He now felt dejected, and wondered why he bothered.

*   *   *

Digby's melancholy lasted for several days. His enthusiasm and passion had been severely impacted by the events of the previous Sunday. He didn't even peruse his *Miller's Antiques Handbooks,* which he often did to while away an enjoyable hour or so.

Digby happened to be reading the local paper, when he saw there was an antiques auction coming up the following week, with viewing on the day before. It gave him pause for thought. It wouldn't hurt to go along and just have a look, would it? It wouldn't do any harm, and at least he could be certain that the antiques would be bona fide and wouldn't get snapped up before anyone else had a chance to look.

Yes, it was a plan; his interest had been rekindled!

* * *

So, it was a rejuvenated Digby who eagerly set off for the auction house that Thursday morning, with his wife's customary warning echoing in his head. On entering the building, he bought himself a catalogue so he could find out the estimated guide price together with a brief description of each item; invaluable should something catch his eye.

He started off by going up and down each aisle, having a quick look to see if anything readily stood out, before going round again and looking properly. There were several nice pieces of porcelain which caught his eye, as well as some Tunbridgeware. Then he noticed a glass vase with a winter scene; it was absolutely gorgeous. Digby picked it up for a closer inspection. He didn't really know anything about glass. The only name he knew was Lalique, but he knew enough to know this wasn't by him. He looked on the base of the vase for any marks and saw the words "Daum Nancy" – it meant nothing to him. He put the vase down and opened his catalogue to see what it said about lot 173.

Apparently, it was a Daum cameo glass vase, with a

guide price of £600 - £700. But it really was beautiful. Digby took out his pen and put an asterisk next to it.

One to think about.

He continued to browse, and saw a few more things he would have liked to own, but, unfortunately, he didn't have very deep pockets. After looking at the paintings, Digby returned to have another look at the glass vase. He couldn't decide whether he dare go for it or not. Already, he could hear the vitriolic diatribe of his wife ringing in his ears, should he go home with it. But the sale wasn't until tomorrow, so he could take some time to think it over.

When he got home, Digby looked through his *Miller's* to see if there was any Daum glassware. He read that Daum glass was set up in 1878 by Jean Daum in Nancy, France. He had experimented with different techniques to produce the beautiful glassware. There were a few examples of similar vases priced between £6,500 - £7,500.

Wow!

His first thought was, had the auctioneer's slipped up? Was this an opportunity for him to make a killing? The pound signs were already showing in his eyes. Gradually, that old feeling he used to get was coming back. Yes; he was back in the groove once more! Then he decided to check online as well and, perhaps, get more of an idea of its value. There were lots to be had; some were valued up to £17,000 or more.

After looking at them, he came to the conclusion that the vase in the sale was worth somewhere in the region of £6,000 - £8,000. Now the question was, had anybody else spotted the mistake? This could be his chance to redeem his tattered credibility. If he was able to buy it for £700 and then sell it on for £8,000, Anne and Gerry would then look at him in a more favourable light when it came to antiques.

Oh yes!

He was a mover and shaker. This time it would be different; he had done his homework and researched the vase. He couldn't go wrong.

*   *   *

It was a glorious sunny morning that Digby woke up to on the day of the sale. He could feel the buzz of adrenaline coursing through his system. After breakfast and a quick look at the paper, he told Anne that he was off out.

'Where are you going?' she asked.

'I'm just popping out for a while, I won't be long'.

'You're going to that auction, aren't you?'

'I, er, that is to say…'

'What are you after buying? Haven't you learnt your lesson?'

'No; I mean yes. This is different; I've done some research on this glass vase, so I know what I'm doing.'

'Who are you trying to kid? If you come back with more junk, which you've wasted your money on, there will be consequences,' said Anne.

'No, no, that won't happen. If it all goes according to plan, it will be quite the opposite – trust me.'

'Trust you? Since when have things ever gone according to any of your plans?'

'But—'

'I don't want to hear any more about it,' cut in Anne. 'If you come back with anything, you know what will happen.'

Well just you wait and see, he thought to himself. I'll show you something when I get back.

Digby arrived about twenty minutes before the sale was due to commence. He wanted another look at the vase to double-check it was the real McCoy. Then he had a long wait for his lot to come up.

He couldn't control his anxiety as he turned things over in his mind. What if the vase wasn't genuine? Doubts began to creep in as he thought back to the mistake he made with the painting. What if he'd missed something again? What would Anne say? What would she do? It would definitely be curtains for any future forays into the world of antiques, and it could also put paid to his marriage as well.

He looked again in the catalogue at the listing for the vase: *Daum cameo glass vase. Guide price £600 - £700.* Yes, that's right, it's in black and white. There's no mistaking it. But surely, he couldn't be the only one to pick up on it. The room was full of dealers: they were bound to have noticed it.

No, it can't be the real thing; the auction house wouldn't have made that mistake. But mistakes do happen, don't they? As he was all too aware. Digby couldn't afford to get it wrong again; he didn't want to be sold another pup.

And so, his torment went on.

'Right. Now we come to lot 173. A beautiful Daum cameo glass vase,' said the auctioneer.

Digby's heart was in his mouth. He was taking quick, shallow breaths, and his heart was pounding. This was it. The moment he had been anticipating. His eyes were fixed on the auctioneer, ready to catch his attention when he made a bid.

'A nice piece. Who's going to start the bidding? What shall we say, £5,000?'

Digby nearly fainted. £5,000? How can that be? The guide was nothing like that. There's got to be some kind of mistake.

'Thank you, I have five. There's five-two online. Five-four – five-six – five-eight – six thousand with me on commission.'

Digby's head was swimming. He was floundering, swamped by the tsunami of ever-increasing bids reining in from all directions.

'Six-eight at the back, thank you. Seven thousand on the phone. Looking for seven-two.'

There was no way Digby could compete at this level. Whatever was he thinking of? So much for his get-rich-quick scheme.

'Any advance on seven-eight? Was that a bid, sir? Thank you. Eight thousand.'

This was surreal. Digby had to pinch himself to make sure he wasn't dreaming. Obviously, he was right in thinking it was the genuine article, but so did everybody else, apparently, apart from the person who valued it for the catalogue.

'Are we all done then at £8,500? The room's out. The phones are out. Are you all sure now? I'm going to sell on the net for £8,500. Going once. Twice…' and down went the gavel.

It was all over.

Digby looked again at the catalogue in disbelief. It clearly stated £600 - £700. He shrugged his shoulders and shook his head. It irked him; there must be an explanation for this anomaly which had caused him so much grief. Digby approached a porter and asked him why the guide price was only £600 - £700.

'Ah, yes,' said the porter. 'Every man and his dog picked up on that. Quite simply, it was typo. A nought was missed off the end of the figures. It should have read £6,000 - £7,000.

Digby had mixed emotions. On the one hand, he was pleased that he had, in fact, got the true value of the vase correct. But annoyed that the auction house had given him false hope with a typing error. Still, at least he hadn't parted with any money this time; which should please his wife.

* * *

One evening, Digby was scrolling through the oil paintings on ebay, as was his wont, and was amazed at some of the dross offered for sale. Did people really buy this stuff? For once, his wife would have been right – it was tat. There were, however, paintings which were quite acceptable, in the two to three hundred pounds bracket, but nothing of any great quality; that is until he clicked on the next page.

And there it was, *the* John Crome painting he thought he'd bought at the car-boot. He couldn't believe his eyes. What a remarkable coincidence. It was up for auction, and the bidding had reached £1,800. At that price it had to be the original. There was still three days to go, and there were seventeen bidders.

Digby clicked on the painting and then scrolled down to read the description:

A charming study of Ludham, Norfolk, with figures and a horse-drawn cart. This unsigned original oil on canvas is attributed to John Crome 1768- 1821, part of the Norwich School.

Well, that's it, he thought. It has to be the original. It's where I used to live and I've got to have it. He scrolled back up the page to study the picture once more. Digby magnified the image so that he could study the finer detail of the painting – it was exquisite. His heart was all aflutter; he could barely contain himself as he clicked on "submit bid". He entered £2,000 and then hit the button, immediately, it came up on the screen that he was the highest bidder. Digby was jubilant, but told himself not to get carried away, there was still three days to go; anything could happen. The auction was ending on Sunday at 23:37. He would be there at the dénouement for sure.

* * *

After breakfast, the next day, the first thing Digby did was to open up his laptop to check on the painting. Much to his chagrin, he found his bid had been usurped. The painting now stood at £2,100. We can't have that, he said to himself, and promptly entered another bid of £2,200. Magic! He was the highest bidder once again.

At the back of his mind was a potential time-bomb permeating through to the forefront of his consciousness, namely: his wife and what she was going to say if she found out – *when* she found out. Especially as he was planning to spend a lot of money. It didn't bear thinking about. If he was lucky enough to get the painting, he would have to tell her he'd paid a lot less for it. It was a dilemma which would require a great deal more thought on his part.

After the six o'clock news, Digby checked his emails and saw that he had one from ebay, informing him he was no longer the highest bidder, and inviting him to make another bid. It now stood at £2,500, so he made a bid of £2,800. Once again, he became the highest bidder.

'You've spent a lot of time on that computer recently; what are you up to?' said Anne.

'Oh, nothing really, just looking.'

'I know what you're like, you hadn't better be buying anything. You've made two mistakes in the past three weeks or so. Fortunately, it didn't cost you anything, but you might not be so lucky next time. But, then, there isn't going to be a next time, is there?'

'No dear,' came the compliant reply.

Dear oh dear, how on earth was he going to get the painting without the inevitable consequences? Digby really wanted it more than anything and he was determined he was going to have it irrespective of the cost.

* * *

Saturday arrived for Digby with the news that the painting was now at £3,330. He was about to make another bid when it dawned on him, all he was doing was pushing up the price. No, he thought, I'll just monitor the bidding until the dying seconds and then sneak in with a last – and hopefully winning – bid.

Yes. A brilliant idea!

So, Digby checked on the bidding throughout the day, resisting the temptation to place a bid. And that night, when he went to bed, the bidding was at £3,450.

One more day to go.

* * *

The following day was full of hope and expectancy for Digby. His early morning check revealed the painting had increased to £3,600. Jeez, he thought, there are some really serious bidders out there.

He was feeling rather listless and the time seemed to be dragging interminably as he waited for the nitty-gritty of the auction to begin.

'Whatever is the matter with you today? You're restless; for Christ's sake find yourself something to do –

you're driving me crazy. If you want something to do, go and cut the grass before it rains,' said Anne.

Digby thought it would be less parlous to do as she suggested. It would help pass some time and maybe he would get some peace and quiet as well.

Somehow, he managed to get through the day. After the late evening news, Anne said, 'That's me done, I'm off to bed. Are you coming?'

'Er…no. Not just now; I'll be up in a little while.'

'Why? What are you going to do?'

'I'm just going to, er—um…'

'If you're up to something on that computer…'

'No, no, I'm just going to finish reading the papers, that's all.'

'A likely story.' And, with that, Anne disappeared up the wooden hill.

Digby patiently waited for ten minutes to make sure his wife was in bed before he opened his laptop. The painting now stood at £3,800, with forty-three minutes left on the clock. Those forty-three minutes would seem like forty-three hours as the seconds and minutes inexorably drained away. He had to remain vigilant; he mustn't let the prize slip from his grasp.

At thirty minutes and £3,900, Digby thought he might as well make himself a coffee; there was still a way to go yet.

Every minute he kept checking the time, willing the countdown to go faster.

Ten minutes. Ten long, laborious minutes. It seemed like an eternity. Digby clicked on "Submit Bid" and in the relevant box he entered £5,000. And with the little hand on the screen poised over "Submit" he was ready to hit the button to make his bid in the dying seconds.

Six minutes. The bidding went up to £4,200. He held his nerve as the tension mounted. Agonisingly, the seconds were ticking away in a long, protracted manner. His breaths were becoming short and laboured.

Three minutes. His heart rate was increasing and he was beginning to perspire. He'd never experienced anything quite like this before.

Two minutes. The top bid was still £4,200. Digby was expecting a sudden flurry of bids to come through, but he still managed to hold his nerve.

Thirty seconds. Still no movement. He stared fixatedly at the seconds as they counted down, trying hard not to blink.

Fifteen seconds. He thought his heart was going to burst; it was going like a steam hammer. He had his index finger poised on the button of his mouse ready to strike. The seconds were relentlessly passing by in slow motion. It was like a Chinese water torture.

Twelve – eleven – ten – nine – eight. Digby hit the button with all the force of a hammer coming down on a nail. The screen went berserk as a succession of bids rained in. For several seconds he had no idea if he'd won. Different images were successively flashed up on the screen in fractions of a second; too fast for him to read.

The culmination of his meticulous planning, and the physically draining anxiety, were all tied up in those few seconds. Digby closed his eyes, he couldn't look. It was too much for him. He couldn't bear the thought that he might have lost out after everything he had put into this endeavour.

Very gingerly, he opened his eyes and there it was: "Congratulations, you won with a bid of £4,845". He'd done it! He savoured the moment. As a great wave of relief washed over him, he slumped back in his chair. Digby was completely drained. At long last he had got it right. He did know what he was doing.

Eventually, he clicked on "Pay Now" to make his payment via PayPal. All done. Delivery was three to five days. All he had to worry about now was, what he was going to tell his wife.

What had he done? That was a lot of money to spend on a painting, even one he felt he had a connection with. It had nearly cleaned him out. But it was too late now, the deal was done. He couldn't do anything about it.

But his wife could!

* * *

Over the course of the next three days, Digby was preoccupied with his thoughts of the impending doom which would prevail once the painting arrived. He had to come up with something – but what? Maybe he could appeal to her better nature; but, then again, he wasn't so sure his wife had one. Perhaps he could tell her he'd bought it for her as an early birthday present. But, no, that was a bit weak and flimsy and would lack any credibility. He could always come clean and then start looking for somewhere else to live!

That wasn't as preposterous as it sounded.

He only had today to come up with something; he'd been advised the parcel would be delivered between nine o'clock and one o'clock the next day. Now, if he could get her to go out in the morning, he would be able to hide the painting, which would then give him more breathing space to come up with a solution.

It was a plan.

Try as he might, Digby was struggling to come up with a suggestion in order that his wife would have good reason to go out. If he was to offer to treat her to a new dress or something, she would immediately suspect he had an ulterior motive. As if.

It was late afternoon when the phone rang. Anne looked at Digby and he looked at her.

'I'm not getting up,' he said. 'It's bound to be for you, anyway.'

'One of these days…' said Anne, as she got up and went into the hall to answer it.

'Hello?'

'Hi Anne. It's Lissie.'

'Oh, hello, how are you?'

'I'm fine, thank you. Yourself?'

'Yes, I'm good.'

'I'm sorry to trouble you, but I'm in a bit of a fix. Claire has had to go home as she's not feeling so good, and tomorrow we've got a funeral. So, I was wondering if you fancied doing a morning shift? I'll pay you, of course.'

'Yes, of course. I'd be only too pleased to help. I told you, when I retired, to call me if you ever needed help.'

'That's great. Thank you so much; you're a life saver. I'll see you in the morning then. Bye.'

'Bye.'

'Who was that?' said Digby, as Anne sat down.

'If you had got up to answer it, you would have found out.'

'I said it would be for you.'

'It was Lissie.'

'Lissie?'

'Yes, Lissie. You know; *Felicity's Flowers?'*

'Oh, right. What did she want?'

'One of the staff has gone off sick, and she wanted me to help her out in the morning. You don't mind, do you?'

Fate had intervened.

Mind? Do I mind? thought Digby. This is manna from heaven. Maybe there is a god after all. It couldn't have worked out any better if I'd planned it.

'No, no, I don't mind. It'll do you good to get out for a bit.'

'What will you do?'

'Oh, don't worry about me. I'll be all right. No doubt I'll find something to do.'

'That's what worries me. There's no telling what you'll get up to behind my back.'

* * *

The following morning, with Anne packed off to work, Digby waited for his delivery to arrive. He had mixed feelings about it. On the one hand, he was excited by the prospect of receiving this wonderful painting which he never expected to get. And on the other hand, there was the problem of his wife's acceptance of the fact, he'd bought it behind her back, and, also, he'd paid a lot of money for it.

As the morning progressed, he kept looking out of the window, anxiously waiting for the delivery to arrive. It got to eleven o'clock and still there wasn't any sign of it.

Periodically, he would go outside to see if the delivery van was anywhere in sight.

At noon, he was starting to get panicky. Not only was he looking for the delivery man, he was now looking out for his wife returning as well.

Then, at twelve-thirty, a van pulled up outside his house. It was here! Digby rushed to open the door and anxiously waited for the man to bring him his parcel. He had a furtive look up and down the road for signs of his wife; wishing the driver would hurry up. It was cutting it a bit fine; she would be back any minute.

'Parcel for Mr. Smythe?' said the driver, as he approached.

'Yes, yes, that's me.'

'There you go then,' he said, handing over the parcel. 'Have a nice day.'

Have a nice day? thought Digby. If only you knew.

Digby hurried back inside and frantically tried to unwrap the parcel. It had yards of tape binding it, so he had to get his Stanley knife to cut through it. The anxiety was increasing as he desperately tried to free the painting from the packaging. His wife would be home any moment. He had to quickly put the packaging straight in the wheelie bin so she wouldn't see it.

Back in the house, he picked up the painting to have a quick look. Oh, yes, it was superb, and it was his! He studied it, grinning from ear to ear. It had been worth all the subterfuge and the nervous tension. He turned it over to look at the verso and very gradually his face turned from one of happiness to one of shock. Digby stared in horror at the thirty-six GALVANISED nails fixing the canvas to the stretcher.

He let out a loud howl.

'Where did that come from?' said a voice from behind. A voice he knew only too well. A voice that sent shivers down his spine.

'I—I—' spluttered Digby, as he slowly turned to face his wife.

'Well? Where did you get that from? And don't you dare lie to me.'

'I wouldn't do that.'

'Right, so, tell me, then.'

'Er—I—er—um—I—I got the painting back from Gerry.'

Who Benefits?

'This looks like the place,' Simon said to himself, as he pulled off the road and into the car park of the Bucket and Spade in the village of Melton. As he got out of the car, the icy wind of the January evening jagged his face.

Walking into the pub, he was hit by a wall of warmth from the roaring log fire. There were perhaps a dozen or so people in there, and they all turned to see who had just walked in.

'You born in a barn?' one said.

'Put the wood in the hole,' shouted another.

'Sorry,' Simon quickly closed the door to keep the heat in. He walked up to the bar and studied the choice of real ales.

'What's your pleasure?' said the barmaid.

Simon looked up to see an attractive woman about 30 years of age smiling at him.

'You'll have to watch her,' said the man behind the bar, 'she's always asking men suggestive questions.'

'Take no notice of George,' she said. 'Now, what do you fancy?'

'See, she's doing it again!'

'Depends on what we're talking about,' said Simon, with a mischievous grin.

'To drink.'

'Oh, okay. What do the locals drink? That's always a good indication of which beer to try.'

'We sell a lot of Brain Stopper.'

'Okay, then I'll have a pint of that, please. Does it work?'

'Does what work?'

'Brain Stopper.'

'Oh, I see what you mean. Well, if some of the locals are anything to go by, I would say, yes, it does. And with an ABV of 6.3% you don't have to drink too much of it before it has the desired effect.'

'Right, thanks. I'll bear that in mind.'

As she pulled the pint, she said, 'I don't recall seeing you in here before, are you new to the area?'

'No. I mean, yes. I'm working in the area for a few days.'

'Oh, yes, doing what?'

'I'm afraid it's all hush hush.'

'Sounds very intriguing.'

'Oh, believe me, it is. If I were to tell you, I'd have to kill you. Keep the change, er…?'

'Trish, and thank you.'

'Pleased to meet you, I'm Simon.'

He took his pint and sat beside the inglenook so he could feel the warmth of the fire and have a good view of the room.

'What do you make of our Trish, then?' Simon turned to see an elderly man with a big, bushy beard. 'If only I was 40 years younger....'

'Yes, I know what you mean, but you've always got your dreams, haven't you?'

'That's all I have got now, dreams and memories,' sighed the old man.

Simon was really savouring his pint; the silky-smooth liquor sliding effortlessly down his throat. It was certainly strong stuff, but it didn't prevent him from going back for another.

'You're brave,' said Trish, as she began pulling him another pint.

'How's that?'

'Well I did warn you about the effects of drinking too much of it.'

'I'm sure I can handle it.' Simon gave her the once over as she pulled his pint. Her shoulder length blonde hair neatly framing a pretty face, and a slightly upturned nose was perched above a generous mouth, 'Will you have one with me?'

'Thank you, I'll have a gin and tonic, if that's okay.'

Simon's lecherous eyes followed the contours of her body as she turned to the till, lingering on a perfectly formed bottom, which was displayed to its best advantage by her skin-tight jeans.

'There you go,' said Trish, handing him his change before getting herself a gin and tonic. 'I don't know if I ought to have this, I've already had two this evening. I don't want to get tipsy because there's no telling what might happen.'

'Now it's you who is full of intrigue. I'd love to know what sort of things you do. Maybe I'll get to find out.'

'Well, it's just that sometimes things get on top of me. I'm struggling to bring up two kids on my own because their father – the useless turd - buggered off a long time ago and doesn't pay me any maintenance. So, things are tough. It's a constant cycle of feeding and clothing the kids, endless housework and pulling pints. So once in a while it's good to let my hair down and have some fun; you know, just to break the monotony.'

'So who looks after the children when you're working?'

'My dear old mum and dad. When I'm working evenings, the kids have a sleepover at their house, which makes it handy if I want to take someone home. Not that it happens very often but I don't want them to have a stream of "uncles" passing in and out of their lives. God, whatever does that make me sound like?'

'It's okay, I understand what you're saying.'

Trish moved to serve another customer. 'Yes love, same again, is it?'

Simon picked up a paper which was on the bar, and was looking at it when Trish returned. 'Is this the local rag?'

'Yeah, there's a bit in there about a prowler who's been following lone women in the area. Everyone is worried and frightened about going out on their own. We don't know when he's going to strike next. George has been taking me home at night, after work, just to be on the safe side'

'Good. You can't be too careful. You never know who it might be.'

'You enjoying your drink?'

'Yeah, it's really something else this beer. But I don't think I'll have another, you were right about its effect.'

'It's seen off many a seasoned drinker before now, isn't that right, Bert?' she called out to the whiskery old man.

'What's that you're saying, my lovely?'

'Just saying how strong Brain Stopper is.'

'Oh yeah, it's strong, right enough.'

Simon enjoyed the rest of his pint whilst the pair continued to flirt.

'What is it going to be now - a soft drink?' teased

Trish.

'What kind of a man do you think I am?'

'I don't know, I'm yet to find out,' said Trish, with a twinkle in her eye.

Oh yes, thought Simon, she's falling for the old charm. It never fails to work. 'Look, when you get a break, why not come and sit with me, then maybe you'll get to find out.'

'Okay. George, is it all right if I take my break now?'

'Yeah, but be you careful,' he said, staring at Simon.

'Great, I'll have a pint of Broadside and get yourself another G&T'

'So, tell me a bit about yourself,' said Trish, as she sat down. 'Are you married? Do you have a partner?'

'Oh, no, footloose and fancy free - that's me'

'That's always good to know; two peas in a pod - me and you. What do you do for a living? 'Sounds like you do a bit of travelling.'

'Yes, but it pays not to tell people what I do.'

'You're not the taxman are you? I could see why you wouldn't want anyone to know that.'

'No, I'm not the taxman,' replied Simon, hoping she would drop the subject 'You really are a lovely girl, you know.'

'You're only saying that because it's true,' she said, the alcohol beginning to take effect. 'But you're not so bad yourself when it comes down to it.'

They became more and more engrossed with one another, it all seemed to be going swimmingly until Trish noticed George holding out his arm and tapping his watch.

'All right, I'm coming, I'm coming. Keep your hair on.'

'It seems like your break is over, just as we were getting to know each other,' said Simon.

'Yes, it's been lovely, thank you.'

'Perhaps we could continue later?'

'Er...yeah, okay, why not?' she said, as she got up and went back behind the bar.

'You seem to have hit it off with our Trish,' said old Bert, with a knowing wink.

'Yes, we were getting along just fine.'

Simon thought back to previous occasions when he was in a similar situation. If his bosses ever found out what he'd done... Well, it didn't bear thinking about. Maybe it was the thought of being caught which gave it an edge, adding to the thrill.

'Last orders, please,' bellowed the landlord.

Simon walked up to the bar to speak to Trish. 'One for the road?' she said.

'No, that's the problem. I've drunk too much to drive, so if you wanted to go into town we'll have to get a taxi.'

'Okay, leave it to me, I've got their numbers.'

'Right, while you are doing that, I'll have another pint

please.'

Trish tried three taxi firms in between serving last orders.

'I can't get a taxi for two hours, would you believe?'

'That's no good,' said Simon. 'So, I suppose the evening is off, then? But I have to get back to my hotel in town, what am I going to do?'

'Well, you could come home with me and try again later to get a taxi.'

'Thanks, that would be great. Sure you don't mind?'

'I wouldn't have offered if I did.'

'Will it be all right to leave my car outside till the morning?'

'It will be fine. Right, I'll just help George to clear up and then I'll be ready to go.'

As Simon went and sat down to wait for her, Trish said to George, 'It's okay, I won't need a lift home tonight, Simon is going to walk me home.'

'What the hell are you playing at? There is something not right about him. You don't know anything about him - he's a stranger. He could be the man who's been following women, and here you are inviting him back to your home. What are you thinking of?'

'I'm a big girl now and I can take care of myself. Besides, I'm sure he's perfectly harmless. What could go wrong?'

'What indeed? Well, you've got my number if you need

it.'

'Okay, thanks George. I know you're only looking out for me.'

As they were about to leave, George handed Trish some money. 'There you go,' he said, 'your wages for tonight.'

'Thanks, I need that.'

'I'm sorry, but I can't offer you a proper nightcap,' said Trish, when they got back to her house. 'My budget doesn't stretch that far; however, I can make us a nice hot, milky drink if you'd like one.'

'Yes, thanks, that would be great.'

As Trish disappeared into the kitchen, Simon looked around the room, which was clean and tidy, and modestly furnished. On a cabinet, there were photographs of a young boy and girl which he assumed must be her children.

'You can put some music on if you like. Have a look and see if there's anything to your taste.'

Simon got up and looked through her collection of CDs before choosing one and loading it into the machine.

'There you go,' said Trish, placing two mugs on the coffee table before sitting down beside him. The faint, rhythmic sound of a beating heart was coming from the speakers. 'So, you're a Pink Floyd fan. I just love this, it's so relaxing.'

'Yes, it is,' said Simon. 'The perfect end to the day.'

As they listened to the music, the small talk got less and less. Trish leaned on Simon and he put his arm around her as the music wafted over them.

The sound of a beating heart gradually petered out, signalling the end of the music.

'That was lovely,' said Trish.

'Yes, but I guess it's time to call a taxi,' Simon said, half-heartedly.

'You don't have to, you know, you could always stay.'

'I thought you'd never ask.'

'So you had it all planned did you?'

'No, no. But I was kind of hoping, I suppose. I really do fancy you.'

'I hope this isn't going to be a one-night stand.'

'Me too. I'd love to see more of you.'

Trish stood up, took his hand, and led him upstairs without saying another word. In the bedroom they sat on the edge of the bed looking at each other, and very tentatively, they moved in for a kiss. Gradually it increased in passion and they were soon undressing each other, tossing their discarded clothes on the floor.

'Let's get into bed; it will be warmer,' said Trish.

Once their pent-up passion was spent, they collapsed and drifted off into a blissful contented sleep.

* * *

It was just after 8 o'clock the next morning when Trish woke up. She looked at Simon and smiled as she remembered the night before. He lay there still in a deep sleep with an arm around her. Very carefully, she extricated herself without disturbing him and went to have a shower.

When she returned, she started to pick up the assortment of clothes strewn over the floor. As she picked up Simon's jacket, his wallet fell out. Trish picked it up and couldn't resist the temptation to look inside, where she found a photograph of Simon and a woman together with two children.

So he is married, she thought, he's not free and single after all. Then she noticed, what looked like, some sort of ID card, so she took it out to have a proper look.

'Shit! what the— You bastard!' she shouted.

At which point, Simon woke up. 'W…What's the matter?'

'What's the matter? You two-faced little shit. What the hell is this?' she said, brandishing the card. 'It says Simon Reed, Benefit Fraud Investigator.'

'H…..Hold on, just hold fire for a moment - I can explain.'

'Oh, I bet you can. You were checking up on me in the pub last night, and don't you dare deny it. And to think I brought you home and we… we …You're also married with children.'

'Look, yes, okay, I admit I was investigating you initially, but what happened between us was all genuine on my part.'

'Oh, I see, you wanted to have your cake and eat it - is that it? Well, I'll tell you something, Mr Simon Bastard Reed, Benefit Fraud Investigator, if you report me, I'll make sure you go down with me. I'm sure your bosses would like to know what happened last night. Now get the fuck out of my house!' And with that she stormed out of the room.

It was half an hour later, as Trish was having her breakfast, that Simon came down the stairs.

'Look, I'm really sorry about what's happened. You can rest assured I won't be filing a report or taking the investigation any further.'

'You wouldn't dare, now get out of my house; I've got to leave in a few minutes for an appointment and I want you gone.'

'Well, look, I could give you a lift - it's no trouble.'

'I'll bet it isn't. There is a perfectly good bus service into town from opposite the pub; now do one.' With that, Trish got up and held the door open for him to go.

Five minutes later when Trish left the house, she found Simon waiting outside the gate.

'What are you waiting for? I've said all I've got to say.'

'I know, but, the thing is, I'm not sure how to get back to collect my car.'

'Well seeing as I've got to go there, I can't stop you following me, can I? More's the pity.' And, with that, Trish set off at a brisk pace with Simon following.

As she approached the main road, the bus went past the junction. 'Damn!'

'Was that your bus?' said Simon as he stopped beside her.

'Yes. Now I'm going to miss my appointment.'

'No you're not, come on, let me give you a lift.'

'If you think I'm getting in that car....'

'Look, no strings, I'm just offering you a lift so you don't miss your appointment. Pure and simple.'

Trish stood there weighing up the situation. The next bus wasn't for two hours, and it was going to hurt her pride, but she said, 'Okay, but I'm warning you, any funny business and...'

'They'll be no funny business,' said Simon.

During the journey into town, Simon tried to make conversation but was met with a stony silence until they got to the outskirts of town.

'Where would you like me to drop you off?'

'At the hospital, please.'

'Whereabouts is that?'

'Further along this road on the left.'

Simon pulled up outside the entrance and said, 'What's

your appointment for? Are you all right?'

'No, not really,' she said, with a smile. 'I've got a follow-up appointment at the clap clinic.'

Hello Darkness My Old Friend

Are you up there, David, somewhere amongst all those stars? It's me, Angie, but I guess you already know that. Do you remember the times when we used to come here together and gaze at all the stars?

The moonlight is dancing upon the water; could that be you I see smiling down on me? As I look up to the night sky, it is alive with a myriad of sparkling crystals. I gaze up at it all and wonder about the vastness which overwhelms me, it's just too much to comprehend.

It's now been some time since you passed away, but you still live on in my heart and my soul. We may have been together for only 10 years or so, but what a decade it was! You were so avant-garde as you went searching for that certain *je ne sais quoi*, which would propel you to stardom. I would like to think I helped you achieve those dizzy heights. I did what I could, like helping you to get a recording contract when I worked for Mercury Records. I also tried to bring some semblance of order to your chaotic life.

Do you remember when we got married in 1970? Mainly because it was mutually beneficial, inasmuch as it cleared the way for you to get a green card to work in America and I would be able to stay here in the UK. We were both very young and idealistic back then, but did we really know what we were doing?

But the success of your endeavours inevitably led to a lot of excesses, be it drink, drugs or sex. Yes, I knew about it, you didn't exactly try to conceal it, did you? So, in a way, I suppose I condoned your hedonistic lifestyle.

But through it all you became a star every bit as luminescent as those I'm now looking at. To your fans you were a messiah, especially when you created Ziggy Stardust, the hermaphrodite alien with red hair. There were, however, times when you appeared to be something of a lost soul, as you went searching for direction and inspiration.

I can see you now, up there with Mick Ronson. You coming up with ideas and him working his magic with the music; you were a great team. It would be nice to think you were both still getting it together.

Hey, do you remember when we lived in that flat in Haddon Hall? It was something of an open house, with people drifting in and out, a bit like our marriage, I suppose. When I think back to all the parties we used to have as well.... But what really annoyed the neighbours most were the rehearsals you used to have with The Spiders. They certainly were happy, heady days.

After years of esoteric reinvention, during which you had several different personae, it was only a matter of time before you were approached to star in films. You made several, some of which were relatively successful, it was just a natural transition for you to make. As I recall, you starred with Catherine Deneuve, Susan Sarandon and Patsy Kensit, to name but a few. You even had a part especially written with you in mind in "Merry Christmas Mr Lawrence". It seemed like everything you touched turned to gold.

But it wasn't just work where you tried to attain a higher plane, it was in your spiritual life too. I remember you studying Buddhism seriously in the early days, when you were trying to get yourself established, and giving some thought to joining a monastery. And then, again, in later life, you considered retiring to a monastery on some misty mountain in Kyoto.

If Buddha was right, then I guess you're not hearing this, as you would have been reincarnated by now. Who knows? Maybe where you are now is the Zenith you were ultimately working towards. There's just so much I don't know. There's never any proof, so how can we be sure which path to follow? Did you know?

Wow! There's a shooting star. You're supposed to make a wish, aren't you? My wish would be for us to be reunited up amongst all those stars. Do you remember how you would always point out which star was which as we lay here drinking in the vast expanse of the night sky? I really cherished those times we spent watching and dreaming as time inexorably slipped by. It felt as if we were the only people alive who understood and appreciated the silent, magical display in the darkness of the universe. You see, it is possible to expand your mind without the use of drugs. Reality can be just as mind blowing if you allow it to.

Lying here, absorbing the enormity of the Cosmos and talking to you, is strangely cathartic. Inasmuch as I feel your presence, everything else has gone from my mind. I am being drawn towards you, nothing else matters anymore. I am in tune with the universe and I feel at one with the spirits. It is overpowering me and I can't help being drawn closer and closer.

It's quite an ethereal experience, but I know everything will be all right and there's nothing to fear. I feel myself inexorably ascending in this brilliant, white light. I am in a kind of vortex, rising smoothly and effortlessly up towards this welcoming nirvana, where I will be reunited with you.

You are waiting for me, aren't you? Everything is just so peaceful and serene, all my problems and worries are behind me now. Ahead is something so beautiful I feel there aren't any words to describe it - to do it justice. It all seems so natural and tranquil, that I don't have to question it, I know it's meant to be.

Are you there David, can you see me? There's not much further to go now. The radiance of the heavenly light is becoming evermore brighter. I can't wait to see what my destiny will be when I have ascended into the blessed state. Is that music I can hear? It's not like anything I've ever heard before.

My senses are becoming dull and at the same time, I'm being enveloped by this dense, smothering fog. I can't get my breath, I can't see. Help me, David. What's happening to me? It shouldn't be like this. No! No! I'm slipping back. I'm not going to make it, I'm powerless to stop it.

'Angela? Angela! Can you hear me? Oh, thank goodness, you've come back to us. For a moment there I thought we had lost you. Everything is okay, you're going to be fine, though it was a bit touch and go for a while. An ambulance is on the way and there's nothing to worry about.'

Nothing to worry about? My attempt to join David has been thwarted. I was so close to being there, so close to joining him in perpetuity. As I ruminated over what might have been, a tear gently rolled down my cheek as I heard the distant wailing of a siren… was I really being saved?

When Love Turns Sour

'Hello? Emma Foster.'

'It's me, Maddie.'

'Oh, hi Sis. What's the matter? You sound upset.'

'I am. It's awful. I don't know what I'm going to do.' And then the floodgates opened; Maddie could no longer hold back the tears.

'It's him again, isn't it? What's that bastard Jason done now?'

'He— He's really gone and done it this time; I wasn't good enough for him,' sobbed Maddie.

'Okay, take deep breaths, and, in your own time, tell me what's happened.'

'The coward didn't even have the balls to tell me to my face: he did it with a text.'

'Did what with a text?'

'Dumped me. Told me he's been seeing someone else

for some time and they're having a baby. And to think, when I was pregnant, he made me have a termination.'

'I'm really sorry to hear that. Honestly, I could swing for him,' said Emma. 'Do you know who the other woman is?'

'Chrissie somebody or other; manages one of his betting shops.'

'If I ever get my hands on him, I'll—'

'I know. I know. I should have listened to you, but I really loved him despite all the stunts he's pulled in the past.'

'Look, why don't you come over and have dinner with us? Nial and Josh would love to see you. You know you're Josh's favourite aunt.'

'No, I wouldn't be very good company right now, and I wouldn't want Josh to see me upset, but thanks anyway.'

'You can't be all alone in your flat at a time like this: I'll pop over after dinner, okay?'

'Yes…okay, if you really don't mind. Thanks.'

It was approaching 8 o'clock when Emma pulled up outside Maddie's flat, and when she opened the door, gone were the sparkling blue eyes that normally greeted people. They had been replaced by eyes which were red and puffy. Her usually immaculate eye make-up was now streaked down her face, and the neat blonde bob which framed her face was now dishevelled. Emma reached out and gave her sister a hug, which brought forth another torrent of tears.

'Okay, Babe, just let it all out. We can overcome this.'

As they sat side by side on the sofa, Maddie said, 'How can I love him, yet, at the same time want to kill him?

'I can understand you wanting to kill him, but not why you love him after all that he's done. It's not as if it's the first time he's cheated on you, stood you up, or messed you around. What about the time he was supposedly taking you away for your birthday, and what happened? He left you high and dry, waiting to be picked up.'

'Yes, but that was due to the pressure of work.'

'Pressure of work, my arse. He has people paid to take the pressure,' said Emma. 'And he didn't even have the decency to call and let you know. He just left you waiting and wondering. That's how much he cares about you.'

'Well…'

'And what about the times he's humiliated you in public; the times when he's had too much to drink and tried to cop off with the busty barmaid? I've seen it with my own eyes; he makes my blood boil.'

Maddie's tears gradually subsided and were replaced with the sniffles. It was all true what Emma had said, but the truth was, Maddie never saw it, or maybe didn't want to. She thought back to the times when they'd been out with a group of friends and Jason would ridicule her, making her the butt of his jokes. Much to his merriment and that of his friends.

'Deep down, I know what you're saying is true, and I really would like to see him pay for all he's put me through.'

'Now you're talking my kind of language, Sis. Let's put our heads together and see what we can come up with.'

* * *

The following evening, Emma phoned Maddie to check she was okay.

'I'm not too bad,' said Maddie.

'How was work?'

'I was doing okay until I received another text from Jason, demanding the return of my engagement ring. How petty is that, coming from a man who's not exactly short of a bob or two? He said he would take "steps" to get it back if necessary.'

'What did you say?'

'I told him to swivel,' said Maddie.

'Good for you, but why is he ratcheting up the ante? Talk about rubbing salt into the wound.'

'God knows. I've got some of my belongings at his, and I need to get them back. Fat chance of that, now, I suppose. Though it wouldn't surprise me if he were to throw them out of the window. It would be par for the course.'

'Any more thoughts of how we can exact revenge?'

'No, but I'm sure you'll come up with something, you normally do.'

'Okay. Do you feel like coming to dinner tomorrow when you finish work?'

'Yes, I'd love to,' said Maddie. 'Thanks.'

* * *

'Have you heard the news?' said Emma, when Maddie arrived for dinner the next day.

'No, I've been at work all day; why, what's happened?'

'They found the body of a man in Harewood Court apartments this afternoon.'

'What? No, it can't be, can it? Do you really think it could be Jason?' said Maddie.

'That's where he lives, isn't it?'

'Yes. Did they give any details?'

'No, they just said the police were conducting their enquiries; talking to residents and appealing for anyone who saw anything to come forward. Is it too much to hope for?' said Emma.

'It wouldn't be anything he didn't deserve, but let's not build our hopes up. It might not be him anyway.'

'Yes, you're right. Nial shouldn't be long, why don't you go upstairs and say hello to Josh? He's been waiting to show you what he did in school today.'

It was during dinner that Nial said, 'Sorry to hear about you and Jason.'

'Thanks,' said Maddie. 'It was probably for the best. I'm now beginning to realize what a fool I've been, putting up with him for so long. And now there's a possibility he may be dead.'

'Yes, so I heard. But in all honesty, I never did think he was good enough for you.'

'That's very kind of you to say so, but, nonetheless, it's not going to be easy to get over.'

'We'll help you all the way,' said Emma. 'You can count on us.'

* * *

As Maddie drove to work the following day, she switched on the radio just in time to catch the local news.

> *"Police have confirmed they are treating the death of a man, found in Harewood Court yesterday afternoon, as murder.*
> *The police also claim they have a significant lead in the case. The identity of the victim is being withheld whilst the early stages of the investigation are ongoing.*
> *Locally, unconfirmed reports claim the victim* was *the owner of several betting shops.*

> *We will keep you updated throughout the day as news comes in."*

God moves in mysterious ways, she thought, with a smug grin. Jason's death would undoubtedly leave a void in her life, but it was a price she was willing to pay.

As Maddie pulled into the carpark of Bridewell Pharmacological Industries, where she worked as a chemist, she wondered what her work colleagues would have to say. But she needn't have worried, they were very sympathetic towards her, expressing their condolences.

It was just after 10:30 when Maddie was summoned to the departmental head's office, where David Morton was sitting at his desk along with a man and woman whom she didn't know.

'Come in, Maddie,' said David. 'This is D I Forbes and D C Charlton. They would like to have a word with you.'

Maddie's heart was pounding; she knew why they were there.

'Miss Traynor, do you know a Mr. Jason Roberts of Harewood Court, Newton Road?' said D I Forbes.

'Yes, I do, or did do,' she said, in a barely audible voice. 'You don't think I…'

'I would like you to accompany us to the station to answer some questions in relation to the death of Mr. Roberts.'

Maddie's legs turned to jelly. 'But I had nothing to do with that. I don't know anything.'

'If you wouldn't mind Miss.'

'But this is ridiculous.'

'If you refuse to come voluntarily, I will have no option but to arrest you. The choice is yours.'

With that, Maddie followed the police officers to their car and back to the station.

There, she was shown into a room with four chairs and a table.

'Can I get you anything Miss Traynor, a drink perhaps?' said D C Charlton.

'No, I'm fine, thanks.'

As they sat down at the table, Forbes said, 'What was the nature of your relationship with Jason Roberts?'

'He was my fiancé.'

'Was?'

'Yes. We split up on Monday.'

'And two days later he's found dead as a result of a blow to the head; which would appear to have been caused by being struck with a heavy, onyx figurine.'

'What are you suggesting, that I'm responsible? I'm not. I didn't do it.'

'We found a text from you on Mr. Roberts's phone saying, "You bastard. You've gone too far this time. You'll pay for this. I'm going to kill you." Do you deny sending the text?'

'No, of course not. You've got the evidence, haven't you? It was in response to the text he'd sent me, telling me it was over.'

'You made a direct threat to kill him.'

'That was just a figure of speech. I didn't mean it. It was done in the heat of the moment. He had just dumped me for that tart who manages one of his shops. Wouldn't you be angry?'

'Where were you between 10am and noon yesterday?' continued Forbes.

'What? I was at work.'

'You didn't leave the premises at any time during the day?'

'No. Wait a minute. Yes, I did. I had a dental appointment at 10:15; that's easily verified.'

'Where did you go after that?'

'Back to work.'

'Well now, how do you explain the fact you were seen entering Harewood Court yesterday morning at approximately 11am? We have a witness who claims she held the door open for you.'

'No, she didn't. That's not true. Sorry. Oh, I remember now. I did go to his apartment, but nobody held the door open for me.'

'So, you do admit to being there? It's surprising how a witness can suddenly jog a memory.'

'I admit to going there but I never went inside his apartment.'

'Why not?'

'Because there was no reply when I knocked on the door.'

'Do you not have a key?'

'Er…yes, I do.'

'So, why didn't you use it?'

'It didn't seem right under the circumstances.'

'And what might they be?'

'I was no longer his fiancé.'

'What was your reason for going there?'

'To collect some things belonging to me.'

'Was this in agreement with Mr Roberts?'

'No.'

'So, you didn't let yourself in and hit Mr Roberts over the head with an ornament?'

'No. Definitely not.'

'But you, Miss Traynor, had a strong motive for killing him. There's evidence you threatened to do so; you had the opportunity, and there's a witness who puts you at the scene. All of which, puts you squarely in the frame.'

'But I keep telling you, it wasn't me and there was no witness. I didn't do it. This is utterly ludicrous.'

'Where are the clothes you were wearing yesterday?'

'In the wash.'

'What do you mean by that?'

'I put them in the washing machine last night before I went to bed. They were ready to hang out this morning before I went to work.'

'How convenient,' said Forbes, 'destroying the evidence.'

'What evidence? There wasn't any.'

'There certainly isn't now.'

'I want to go.'

'All in good time, Maddie. We need to check out your movements; in the meantime, you will be detained in custody.'

'You can't do that.'

'I think you'll find we can.'

'I need to make a phone call.'

'All in good time, Maddie,'

'So, you keep saying. Now is a good time.'

'We'll speak to you again later.'

It was early evening when D C Charlton collected Maddie from her cell and escorted her back to the interview room.

'Well, can I go now?' said Maddie, as she sat down.

'We have reports of a heated argument coming from inside the apartment. What have you got to say about that?'

'Nothing. I didn't hear it.'

'So, after a heated exchange with Mr Roberts, you struck him over the head with a figurine, didn't you?'

'No. I never killed him.'

'What was the argument about?'

'There was no argument. At least, none I was party to.'

'Miss Traynor, you had a strong motive for killing Mr Roberts. There's evidence you threatened to kill him. A witness who puts you at the scene. You had a key to let yourself into the apartment, and you were heard arguing.

The evidence is all there, yet you still maintain it wasn't you and you know nothing about it. Do I look like I was born yesterday?'

'The evidence is all circumstantial,' said Maddie. 'You've got no proof. Now can I go home?'

Through pursed lips, Forbes let out a heavy sigh as he thought things over. 'Okay, we'll leave it there for the time being. You are being released under investigation, so don't go taking any holidays.'

Later that evening, Maddie phoned her sister to tell her of the day's events.

'They really think you killed him?' said Emma.

'Yes, they've got the text I sent threatening to kill him, and a witness who says she saw me enter the building. I've left myself wide open. I swear it wasn't me: I had nothing to do with his death.'

'I know you didn't.'

'But the evidence is stacked against me. Why would the witness say she saw me when she didn't? I just hope they find the person who did do it.'

'They won't, and as long as they don't find out you've got an identical twin sister, they never will.'

A Lack of Honour

'You want me to do what?'

'I think you heard me, Carter.'

Who was this thick-set man with the piercing eyes? How did he know my name? I had only called into the pub for a quiet drink before heading off home for dinner.

'Are you for real,' I said. 'Not only is it impossible but you seem to think I'll do it.'

'Oh, you'll do it alright, make no mistake.'

'You're seriously asking me to retrieve a kilo of cocaine held in Cannon Road Police Station? What on earth makes you think I could, or would, want to do it?'

'I've done my homework on you, Carter. I know you do the odd job here and there, and you're very good at it. I'm also willing to pay you five grand for your trouble.'

'I don't know where you got your information from, but I wouldn't risk my liberty, certainly not for five grand. So, I suggest you toddle off back to where you came from and find somebody else. I'm not interested.'

He stared down his hooked nose, his close-set brown eyes not giving anything away. He pursed his lips as he slowly let out a long, audible sigh.

'I don't think you fully understand the situation,' he said finally. 'I know you've done jobs for acquaintances of mine, now if they were to come to light…need I say more? I know all about Angela Brookes, your bit on the side. How long is it you've been visiting her house in Nelson Street? How can she afford to live there on a secretary's salary? Methinks she's getting some help from her sugar daddy.'

Shit. How did he find out about her?

'Needless to say, if you don't play ball, I will make sure your wife, Jill, gets all the details.'

He had me over a barrel. There was a great deal at stake and I couldn't afford to take the risk of calling his bluff.

'You seem to have done your homework,' I said.

'Oh, I have, believe me. And I'm wondering how you can afford your house on the salary you get, or, for that matter, the nice shiny Lexus you drive. It's patently obvious you have to rely on a "supplementary income" in order to maintain your lifestyle. Now, if the police were to do a bit of digging…'

How could he have found out about all that? I've

always been careful to cover my tracks – or so I thought. I really couldn't afford to have all that coming out; I'd be ruined. I'd lose my job, my house, my wife and my liberty.

'I, er…seem to have little choice, but why go to all that trouble for the sake of some cocaine, why is it so important?'

'It's important because a friend of mine is on remand pending a trial for being in possession of the drug with intent to supply. He is facing a lengthy stretch given his previous. But more worrying, is the fact he might turn queen's evidence, which would mean a few of us would end up in deep shit. But if you were able to – how can I put it? – avail yourself of the evidence, there would be no case to answer. My friend would walk free and we would still have our merchandise, and you, Carter, would be a few grand to the good. It's a win-win all round.'

He was so cool and calm about it, he oozed confidence, knowing he was in the driving seat. But how the hell was I going to obtain the drugs? They were in a police station, for Christ's sake.

'How do you think I am going to be able to pull this off and give you what you want?'

'Not my problem. If it's true what they say about you, you'll find a way. If you don't, then you know what the consequences will be.'

'It's not going to be easy; and I want ten grand for my

trouble. It's worth that if it all goes the way you want it to.'

'Don't push it, Carter,' he said, slamming his glass down on the table. It will be Goodnight Vienna, if you do.'

'And it will be curtains for you, as well, if I don't. Think about it. And don't push me too hard or you'll regret it.'

He was now riled. There was no way of telling which way it would go. He looked down, picked up his glass and drained it. After some thought, he said, 'Okay, ten grand it is, but there hadn't better be any hiccups. I'll call you in a few days and you better have good news for me.'

'I'll call you,' I said, 'when I've got news.'

'Oh, no you don't, Sunbeam, that's not how it works. I call the shots. Now give me your number.'

Reluctantly, I gave it to him, and, with that, he got up and walked out of the pub.

When I arrived home, Jill was cooking the dinner. 'Had a good day, Bob?' she asked.

'Yeah, okay, the usual. You know, same old, same old.'

'That's all you ever say to me. I'd like to know what's happened.'

'I'm sorry, but some days I've just had a gut full of it, and when I get home, I want to leave it all behind and just relax and unwind.'

'Okay, have it your way. Dinner is just about ready; call the kids and get them to wash their hands, will you?'

They came bounding down the stairs; James closely following on the heels of his older sister, Amy.

'Hi Dad! They chorused. 'Are you coming with us to Grandma's at the weekend?'

'Er…I don't think so, Amy. It doesn't look like I'll be able to get away.'

'Oh, not again,' said Jill. 'You know mother always likes to see you. She'll soon begin to think you're deliberately avoiding her. When was the last time you came with us for the weekend?'

'I know, I know. It's just that I've got a lot on my plate at the moment, and then something else cropped up today which I have to deal with. I'm sorry, I will make it up to you as soon as I get things straightened out – promise.'

That evening, I couldn't concentrate, my mind was still on the mystery man. How could I possibly do it? How could I possibly not do it? It didn't bear thinking about. I couldn't work out how he came to know so much about me. It was unsettling not knowing; for once, I didn't feel in control.

'Did you hear what I said,' asked Jill. 'You've been in a world of your own all evening. What's troubling you?'

'Sorry, love. It's just this work thing playing on my

mind.'

'Problem shared…? Thought not. I asked if you would be able to take me and the kids to the station on Friday to catch the train down to Mother's?'

'Yes, I should think so, work permitting. What time does it leave?'

'6.22 pm. Let me know if you can't, so I can book a taxi. Are you sure you can't come?'

'No. I mean yes; I can't possibly make it.'

* * *

The next morning, I was sitting at my desk when my mobile rang. I looked at the screen and saw it was Angela. I screwed up my face, cursing. I had forgotten to call her yesterday.

'Hello,' I ventured. 'Yes, I know I should have called you, but it went clean out of my head. I've had a few problems – still have, as a matter of fact.'

'It's okay, I'm getting used to it. Are we still on for the weekend?'

'Yes, Jill and the kids are going to her mother's on Friday. I've got to drop them at the station, then I'll come straight to yours. I should be there about sevenish, if that's alright?'

'That's fine by me,' said Angela. 'Maybe we can do something – go somewhere. Are you free for lunch today?

Perhaps we could meet at Chico's, where we normally go.'

Maybe that's just what I needed: a bit of distraction. 'Usual time, one o'clock?'

'Yes, and don't you dare be late!' And with that, she hung up.

Angela was a lively, fun girl, who usually managed to lift my spirits but she would certainly have her work cut out today. The thing is, I couldn't tell her about the fix I was in because she knows nothing about that side of me. No one did, apart from those who I've done jobs for, but I was in desperate need of some inspiration to resolve my current difficulties.

As I sat at the table drinking coffee and waiting for Angela to arrive, I watched people toing and froing around the market square. Each going about their day-to-day business, seemingly carefree – what I would give to be one of them.

'I don't believe it. You're actually here before me.'

I looked round to see Angela slipping off her coat.

'Have you ordered yet?'

'No,' I replied. 'I didn't know when you would get here, or what you fancied.'

'Oh, you know me; something light and healthy.'

'I think I'm going to have a jacket potato with chilli. How about you?'

'I'm not so sure that's light and healthy. Oh, what the hell, you only live once – let's go for it.'

As we were eating, I became interested in the comings and goings across the square. I had seen two or three people going up to this guy standing in an archway, then they would disappear into the alcove of the building before re-emerging, and the guy taking up his position once more, leaning against the wall. He was obviously a drugs dealer.

'Hello? Planet Earth to Robert. Are you receiving?'

'I, er…I'm sorry.'

'Honestly, Bob, where are you? You're miles away. More interested in what's happening out there, than you are in me. There's obviously something on your mind – what is it? Is it this work thing you mentioned?'

'Yes, I suppose it is.'

'Well, whatever it is, I hope you soon resolve it because it's clearly weighing heavy on your mind.'

'Actually, I think I might just have a solution to the problem.'

'Good. So, maybe you can now concentrate on me and the food.'

After lunch, Angela and I parted company, going in opposite directions, ostensibly to return to work. Fifty yards later, I stopped and checked that Angela had disappeared from view. I then went across the square to see if the guy I had observed earlier was still there.

He was.

I stood watching, and the same thing happened again when a dishevelled youth approached him.

As I went up to the dealer in the black hoodie and ripped jeans, he looked a bit apprehensive and worried. I wasn't dressed in the same clothing as his other customers.

I said, 'Can I have a word?'

'About what?' His furtive eyes darting up and down the street.

'I want to put some business your way.'

'Oh, yeah, and what business might that be, Grandad?'

'Look, it's okay, I'm not the law. Can we go somewhere out of sight to talk? I don't want to draw any attention and neither do you.'

He nodded his head in the direction of the alcove and I followed him in. Once inside, I said, 'I need a large amount of coke, can you help me?'

'Dunno, depends what you mean by large.'

'A kilo.'

'A kilo? You want a brick? Shit man, that's gonna be one hell of an effing party.'

'Never mind that, can you get it, or arrange for me to get it?'

'Are you serious? Who are you, anyway? You trying to set me up? I don't deal in those sort of quantities; it's above my pay grade.'

'I realise that, but can you arrange something for me? I'm on the level – strictly legit, and I'm not playing games.'

'It'll effing cost you,' he said.

'How much?'

'Dunno, can't really say, but it will be mega-bucks.'

'How long will it take you to get a price and delivery, then?'

'I should be able to find out by tomorrow. Give me your number and I'll call you when I have the info. And just remember, if there's any funny business, there are some nasty, ugly people further up the chain who wouldn't take too kindly to that. Get my drift?'

'Yeah, okay, I understand, but I need it asap.'

I walked away with a sigh of relief: that went better than I had anticipated. If I can get the coke, I will be able to pass it off to Hook Nose as coming from the police station. He will then, in turn, give me my money, which will hopefully reimburse me for what I had laid out. Okay, I wouldn't have made any money but I will have him off my back and everything will be back to normal.

* * *

It was late afternoon the next day, when my mobile rang. I looked at the screen and it revealed the number had been withheld.

'Hello?'

'You don't know me, but you were expecting this call,' the voice said. 'I have something you want and I can supply the full amount.'

'Good, that's brilliant,' I replied.

'It will cost you fifty grand, in readies, naturally.'

'How much? You're having a laugh.'

'Listen, mister, that's the going rate. You either take it or leave it - it's your choice.'

My choice? There really wasn't a choice because if I didn't go through with it, my whole world would come tumbling down.

'Can you raise that kind of cash?' he continued.

'Yes, I suppose I could at a push.'

'So, have we got a deal, then? Do you want to go ahead?'

'Yes, okay. I don't really have much of a choice. When can you deliver?'

'When you've got the money.'

There was no way I could withdraw that amount of cash without loads of questions being asked, and it would be traceable if I did. No. I would have to take it from my safety deposit box, where I kept all the proceeds from my "little earners".

'I can get it by tomorrow. Where and when can we meet?'

'Slow down. First things first. I will give you a call this

time tomorrow to check you've got the readies. Then, and only then, I will give you a time and a place.'

The line went dead.

* * *

The following afternoon, as I drove to the bank, I became aware of a black BMW which had been behind me for some time. Why would anyone want to follow me? Could it be the drugs dealer? No. It didn't make sense. He doesn't know who I am, and what would he have to gain by doing so? It could be Hook Nose, I suppose, keeping tabs on me for some reason.

Time to find out.

At the next junction, I took a sharp left at the last second without indicating. As I straightened up, I looked in my rear-view mirror, only to find my pursuer was still there. So, he was following me, but why? Maybe I should put my foot down and try to shake him off, but that would only attract attention and let my pursuer know I had clocked him. Should I just pull over and see what he does? No. That might lead to a public confrontation and that's the last thing I wanted.

I continued driving whilst I frantically searched for a way to escape my pursuer. Up ahead was a set of traffic lights which turned amber as I approached. I put my foot down and went through, only for the BMW to go through on red. Shit. Who the hell was it? Perhaps I should go somewhere less populated, stop and confront him.

I carried on, sticking to the speed limit and looking in the mirror. The BMW was now tailgating me and there was a woman in the passenger seat. I blinked as the sweat from my brow stung my eyes. What was he playing at? He was going to cause an accident. Why make it so obvious he was following me? None of it made any sense. I touched my brakes to make him back off – it had the desired effect.

As I was passing the hospital, I looked again in the mirror and saw the car veer off, taking the turning for the A&E department. I breathed a heavy sigh of relief: the tension draining from me. He was simply trying to get to the hospital as quick as he could for some medical emergency.

I was becoming paranoid.

I was lucky to get a parking space near the bank; still checking I wasn't being followed. Entering the bank, I looked around to see if there was anybody I knew. I didn't want to have to explain my presence. Satisfied, I made my way towards the steps leading down to the vault. Suddenly, a hand grabbed my shoulder from behind. A vaguely familiar voice I couldn't quite place said, 'Shouldn't you be somewhere else?'

I froze. My heart was pounding. Instinctively, I knew there was going to be trouble. As I slowly turned, I found myself, once again, looking into the piercing eyes of Hook Nose.

'What the f— are you following me, or have you come to get my money? And get your hands off me or I'll—'

'You'll what, Carter? You can't afford to cross me.'

'Maybe not now, but my time will come.'

'You threatening me? I thought we had a gentleman's agreement. Have you got anything for me yet?'

'Keep your voice down,' I hissed. 'I'm working on it.'

'In that case, what are you doing here? The clock is ticking. I'll give you a day or two, then you'd better have some good news for me.'

'Now who's threatening?'

'I'm in the fortunate position of being able to.' And, with that, he turned and went out the door.

What was all that about? Was he just trying to keep up the pressure? There were one or two people giving me a cursory glance, but nothing to worry about. I composed myself and continued heading towards the vault.

I counted out the money twice, just to be sure, then I bundled the notes into an old briefcase, which was less likely to attract attention.

When I got back to my car, I placed the briefcase in the boot, having checked nobody was watching. All I had to do now was wait for the phone call. But there was a problem which was bugging me. I'll have paid out fifty grand for the coke but would only receive ten grand for it when I handed it over. That's one hell of a discrepancy which I was not willingly going to take.

There was also another problem which compounded the issue, one I hadn't given any thought to at the time. As the drugs wouldn't be from the police station, the man on remand wouldn't be released, so Hook Nose would follow through with his threats. I couldn't threaten him with the police because he would take me down with him. So that was a non-starter.

Time was ticking away as I sat ruminating over the problems. If I didn't get Hook Nose some coke, I wouldn't have anything to begin bargaining with.

Then my phone rang.

'Hello?'

'You got the money?'

'Yes.'

'Do you know the multi-storey carpark on Duke Street?'

'Yes.'

'Be on the rooftop level at 7 pm.'

'Okay.'

And the line went dead.

I arrived at the multi-storey just after 7 pm and drove round the helter-skelter which took me to the rooftop. There were three cars parked there, so I reversed back to the wall opposite a black Range Rover with a man sitting behind the wheel. The other two cars were empty, so he must be the one. I didn't move: I waited to see if he gave some sort of signal.

How could I be sure he was the man? Conversely, he wouldn't know if I was the person he was waiting for. How were we going to break this impasse? We were both taking a risk. After a few minutes, there was still no movement, so I thought I would try and sound him out. I casually got out of the car and walked over to the Range Rover. He lowered his window.

'Can I help you?' he said.

'Maybe. I'm supposed to meet somebody here who's got something for me. Would that be you?'

'Maybe. Who are you?'

'None of your business. I'm just another customer, now have you got something for me or not?'

'Like what?'

'Well, if you don't know, then I guess you're not the man I'm waiting for.'

'You could be the Old Bill for all I know.'

'Do I look like the police? If I was, this place would be swarming with cops by now.'

'So, I assume that what ever it is you're looking to buy, must be illegal, is it?'

'Come on, cut the crap. Have you got something for me?'

'You got something for me in return?' he asked.

'Yes, now show me the merchandise.'

'Oh, no. I need to see the colour of your money first.'

'Okay, then I'll get it.'

When I returned to his car, I got in the passenger seat beside him and handed over the briefcase.

'You'll find it's all there.'

He took it from me and, reaching into the case, he flicked through the bundles of notes, doing a rough calculation.

'That seems to be okay,' he said eventually.

'Right, where's the merchandise, then?'

He reached under his seat and brought out a package. 'And you'll also find it's all there.'

I weighed it in my hand as if to check it was a full kilo. 'Right, thanks.' And, with that, I got out of the car and headed back to mine. Now all I had to do was wait for Hook Nose to contact me. But between now and then, I had to come up with a plan to get out of this mess unscathed.

Some hope.

My first priority was to find somewhere to hide the coke. I couldn't afford to be caught in possession of class A drugs. Maybe it would be better if I was to bury it somewhere as there would be less chance of somebody stumbling across it. I was on the right side of town for Chesterton Gorge, so I headed in that direction. There would be plenty of places to hide it in the woods.

There were no cars in the parking area when I pulled into it. As I entered the wood, there was still enough light left for me to see where I was going. I didn't want to go too far in because it would be more difficult for me to find.

I came across a fallen tree which had been uprooted, and there was space between the trunk and the roots just big enough to take the package. Having placed it in position, I covered it with twigs and leaves so it looked natural and couldn't be seen.

But the problem of the man on remand and the cash shortfall, still remained.

It was dark by the time I got home.

'You're late tonight,' said Jill, as I entered the kitchen. 'I've had to give the kids their dinner earlier as they were starving. I've kept ours warm in the oven, so it's ready whenever you are.'

'Sorry love, something came up and I had to deal with it. You know how things are.'

'Yes, I do know, but it would help if, once in a while, you rang to let me know.'

'It's not always possible, sometimes it goes completely out of my mind.'

'Well, I hope you taking us to the station tomorrow, hasn't gone completely out of your mind, too.'

'As if. I'm just going to grab a shower before dinner, if

that's okay with you?'

'Fine. You had better do it now before it goes out of your mind,' she jibed.

* * *

Again, I had another fitful night's sleep as I continued to wrestle with the dilemma. It was no good doing a runner because the outcome would be the same: I would lose everything. I was well and truly buggered.

Most of the day was taken up with writing reports and associated paperwork before I became snowed under by it. I had expected to hear from Hook Nose by now, but maybe that was good news. I knew it wasn't because there was too much at stake. I was bound to hear from him soon. Then, as if by magic, my mobile rang. I took it out of my pocket, only to find it was Jill calling.

'No, I haven't forgotten,' I said, before she had chance to speak.

'Well, I couldn't be sure, so I had to check.'

'I won't be long. I'll be leaving soon, okay?'

'Right, we're all packed and ready to go. See you soon.'

My thoughts turned to the weekend and Angela, but with so much on my mind, I feared I wouldn't be able to make the most of it. If she were to find out, there's no telling how she would react. But, right now, I was the one in a difficult position. I needed to get some fresh air to clear my head, so I left off to go and collect Jill and the kids.

'Well, not only did you remember but you arrived early, as well. How strange is that?' said Jill, as I walked in. 'This calls for a double celebration!'

'I could still make you take a taxi, you know. So just cut the sarcasm or I won't be there to pick you up on Sunday, either.'

'I've left a post-it-note on the fridge to remind you to pick us up just after 8 pm.'

'You really are Miss Efficiency personified, aren't you? Where are your bags? I'll put them in the car.'

'They are all packed and ready to be brought downstairs.'

I fetched the bags and put them in the boot of the car and ten minutes later, we were on our way. And I was that little bit closer to Nelson Street and all the delights within.

I pulled up outside the station and Amy said, 'Are you coming to wave us off, Daddy?'

I looked around and said, 'Sorry, I can't, love, there aren't any parking spaces to be had but I'll be waiting on the platform when you return on Sunday.'

'Promise?'

'Yes, I promise. Now get a move on or you'll miss the

train.'

Jill leaned over for a kiss and said, 'Bye, and don't forget to remember to remember!' and then they were gone.

I eased the car back into the traffic and twenty minutes later I was knocking on Angela's door. When it opened, there stood this ravishingly beautiful woman of thirty-two. Her long blonde hair cascaded down to her breasts, which were covered by an apron.

'Forgotten your key?'

'No, sorry, I didn't think.'

'Well, come in, don't just stand there. Dinner is nearly ready – it's your favourite: beef stroganoff followed by rhubarb crumble.'

God, I must have died and gone to heaven. I closed the door and followed her into the kitchen.

'That smells really good. Can I do anything?'

'You can open the bottle of wine, I've got everything else under control.'

'Including me?' I joked.

'I don't think anybody has you under control.'

'You might be surprised on that point.'

'Nothing about you surprises me anymore. Right, this is now ready. Pass me the plates.'

As we were eating the stroganoff, Angela said, 'Has someone got control of you? You seemed to be troubled about something the other day when we had lunch.'

'Kind of. It is to do with that, but hopefully it will be resolved very soon, one way or another. And before you ask, no, I can't discuss it with you, okay?'

'Oh, get you, Mr Mysterious. Are you able to discuss what we could do this weekend?'

'We can do anything you like – whatever takes your fancy.'

'Okay, maybe we can go for a drive in the country and find a nice pub to have some lunch.'

'Yes, I'd like that. Now, is that rhubarb crumble ready?'

* * *

As we drove along, my mind predictably turned to Hook Nose. What if he rang when I was with Angela, how would I avoid her overhearing the conversation?

'Honestly, you've not heard a word of what I've been saying, have you?'

'Er…no, sorry. I was concentrating.'

'Yes, you were, but not on me or the road ahead. It doesn't take an Einstein to work out what it is. It's that bloody work thing, isn't it?'

'Yes, okay, it is. I'm sorry, but there's a hell of a lot at stake, and if there are repercussions, yours truly would be in very deep shit.'

'Just what are you involved with Bob? What exactly is

at stake?'

'There's no need for you to worry: it will all work out fine.'

'Why don't I believe you?'

'Look, just trust me. Don't let it spoil the day.'

Then, as if on cue, my phone rang. It had to be him.

'Aren't you going to answer that?' said Angela.

'No. I'm driving, in case you hadn't noticed.'

'Well, give it to me, I'll answer it.'

'No. If it's important they'll try again later.'

'You know who it is, don't you?'

'How could I possibly know who it is when the phone is in my pocket?'

'Let me—'

'Just drop it, will you? It's only a bloody phone call,' I said sharply.

'There's no need to speak to me like that, I was only trying to help.'

'I don't need your help, okay?'

The phone stopped ringing and a lengthy silence then ensued.

'I'm sorry, you didn't deserve that. I guess the problems are getting to me more than I realised.'

'Evidently. I don't mean to pry – poke my nose in – but I don't like to see you like this. I just want to help you but you won't let me in.'

'Believe me, you're better off not knowing and you

wouldn't be able to help anyway.'

'If I was in trouble, you would want to help me, wouldn't you?'

'Of course, but this is completely different.'

'Can't any of your work colleagues help? Surely there must be someone you can talk to.'

'Not this time. It's something only I can deal with.'

We drove along for another two or three miles and came to a stop at a railway crossing. My phone rang again.

'If you answered that, the person wouldn't keep ringing,' said Angela.

'I know. I know.' I took the phone out of my pocket and checked to see who was calling. 'Brilliant!'

'Who is it?'

'Dunno. Number withheld,' I said, putting it back in my pocket.

After spending another half-an-hour driving, I suggested we pull into a nice-looking *"Olde worlde"* pub, up ahead, to have some lunch.

'Good, I'm just about ready for something to eat, and perhaps you'll be able to pay me a bit more attention, if your phone ever stops ringing, that is.'

'Sorry, it's just—'

'I know what it's just. Why don't you phone the guy and get it sorted?'

'I haven't got his number.'

As we got out of the car, my phone rang yet again.

'ANSWER IT!' shouted Angela.

'Okay, you go in and grab a table; I'll be with you in a minute.'

'Just get it sorted!' and with that, she headed for the pub.

'Hello?' I said tentatively.

'You know who this is, so I won't introduce myself. Have you got my property back for me?'

'Have you got my money?'

'Yeah, and you can have it as soon as I get what's mine.'

'Right, so we need to meet up to exchange gifts, don't we?'

'That's the general idea,' he said. 'Where are you?'

'None of your business.'

'We need to arrange a time and a place, and the sooner the better.'

I gave the matter some thought and then said, 'I can't make it until 7 pm tomorrow evening because I'm out of town at the moment.'

'S'pose that'll have to do then, won't it?' he said begrudgingly.

'Do you know Chesterton Gorge?'

'Yes, of course I do, what of it?'

'I'll meet you there tomorrow at 7 pm.'

'It's a big place.'

'There's a footpath that runs along the top of the gorge beside the woods. About four hundred yards along the path, you'll find a bench, where people sit and look out over the gorge. We won't be seen there.'

'Listen, Sunshine, I call the shots.'

'I have to go there anyway because that's where I've stashed your stuff. So, it makes sense to meet there.'

'I hope you're not planning any funny business.'

'It's in both our interests to be straight with each other because we know the consequences, don't we?'

'Yeah, okay, you're right, we can't be doing with any of that. I'll see you tomorrow.'

Phew! Now the ball was rolling, and I had just over twenty-four hours to come up with a plan.

When I went into the pub, Angela was sitting at a table with two drinks and a menu.

'All sorted?' she enquired.

'Yeah, well, sort of, I suppose.'

'But—'

'Don't ask,' I said. 'Now, let's get something to eat.'

On the drive back, I continued turning things over in my mind, which, of course, didn't go unnoticed.

'You haven't sorted things, have you?'

'I've sorted part of the problem but there are still complications.'

'I'm sorry, I don't mean to nag you, but I'm worried.'

'There's nothing for you to worry your pretty little

head over, it'll be fine,' I said, with more conviction than I felt. 'I'm meeting him tomorrow and it will all be resolved, one way or another.'

'That doesn't sound very reassuring.'

'What doesn't?'

'One way or another.'

'It's just a figure of speech, you shouldn't read too much into it.'

* * *

It was just after 7 o'clock on Sunday morning when I roused from yet another troublesome night's sleep. It was D day, Do or Die. And I still had no idea how I was going to get round the problems. I got out of bed, shaved and showered, then went downstairs to make some breakfast. I took a tray upstairs for Angela.

'Breakfast is served m'lady.'

'What's all this in aid of?' she said, pulling herself up into a sitting position.

'I thought it would be nice for you to have it in bed for a change. Call it my good deed for the day.'

'Thank you, it's very sweet of you. What do you fancy doing today?'

'Nothing really, I'd just like to chill out, if that's alright with you. I've got to leave about half-five.'

'Half-five?'

'Yes, I've got that bit of business to attend to, and then

I've got to pick Jill and the kids up from the station.'

'Will whatever's been bothering you really be over and done with this evening?'

'For Christ's sake! How many more times have I got to tell you? Just let it drop.'

It was with some trepidation that I set off on my mission. The plan was to get there early in case a reception committee was waiting. As I pulled into the parking area there were no other cars present, which I thought was a good omen. Unless, of course, he or they had entered the gorge from the opposite direction, which would mean a longer walk.

I entered the wood, ever-vigilant in case there was someone watching. With every step came the sound of twigs snapping underfoot, which sounded loud in the stillness of the trees. I soon found the tree and sat on it for a few minutes, looking and listening. Feeling sure there was nobody around, I retrieved the coke and headed for the path which would take me to the rendezvous.

There was still the problem of the prisoner to resolve. Maybe I needed to be more proactive and take matters into my own hands. The circumstances dictated drastic measures, but had I got the bottle?

I arrived at the meeting place a little after 6.30 and looked in the wood, but thankfully there wasn't anybody lurking behind the trees. I walked to the edge of the gorge and looked down into the abyss some three hundred feet below. Feeling a bit giddy, I quickly stepped back and sat down on the bench to wait.

The minutes ticked by interminably as I mulled over every possible scenario. If he was on his own, I felt sure I could handle him. Ten minutes later, I caught sight of a solitary figure in the distance walking towards me. In the failing light, he was too far away for me to identify, but it could only be Hook Nose.

This was it – survival of the fittest.

'You're early.'

'So are you,' I replied.

'Have you got what I came for?'

'Have *you* got what *I* came for?'

'Look, I'm not here to play games. Have you got the coke?'

'Yes, if you've got my money.'

'Give me the coke first.'

I got up from the bench and handed it over. 'Now, where's my ten grand?'

'Did you really think I was going to hand over the money when I've got you where I want you? You can't afford to drop me in it because you've got more to lose than I have.'

'You bastard!' I yelled, moving in on him.

'Not so fast, Sunbeam,' he said, stepping back and pulling out a gun. 'I've got what I wanted and if I take you out of the equation, I have nothing more to worry about.'

It was do or die.

A red mist descended. Instinctively I hurled myself at him, taking him by surprise. He quickly stepped back, and, as he did so, tripped over an exposed tree root, landing on his back. The gun went off and the bullet went into the trees. As he struggled to get up, I kicked him in the head and he went down again. Quick as a flash, I stamped on his hand which held the gun. He squealed and released his grip. I grabbed the gun and stepped back, putting space between us. I pointed the gun at him as he gradually got to his feet.

'Not so clever now, are you?'

'Look I've got your money here in my pocket. Let's talk this through. We can sort it out.'

'We've done all the talking we're going to do.'

'You haven't got the balls to pull the trigger, we both know that,' he snarled.

'You sure about that? If I kill you, I get the money and the coke, and, more importantly, I won't have to live with the knowledge that you've got a hold over me.'

'Come on, we can both have what we want.'

'One more step and you'll get something you don't want,' I replied.

'Look—'

In a cold and clinical manner, I squeezed the trigger. He went down like an Aunt Sally, a bullet hole in his forehead. It was the first time I had killed anyone. I stood in disbelief at what I had done. I had actually killed someone. I started to shake as I processed what had happened. I really didn't have any other choice. It was either him or me.

Now I needed to get away, but first I had to dispose of the body. It took me several minutes to take stock of the situation. I needed to think logically and methodically. First, I put the gun down, then took his phone and removed the sim card, putting it in my pocket to dispose of later. I then hurled the phone way out into the gorge.

So far so good.

I took the money out of his coat pocket and put it in mine. It was amazing how cool-headed I had become. Next, I rolled the body over the edge of the precipice and down into the gorge below. Right, job done. I picked up the drugs and the gun and set off back to my car. Along the way, I threw the gun way out into the gorge, a long way from the body.

I was feeling quite pleased with myself at the way things had turned out. All that remained was to sell the coke and get my money back to add to the ten grand. And the beauty of it all was, nobody knew what had happened.

* * *

The following morning, I was sitting at my desk catching up on the never-ending paperwork, when my boss approached me.

'A body with a gunshot wound has been found by a

dog walker at the bottom of Chesterton Gorge. I want you, D I Carter, to head up the investigation.'

'Right O, Guv, I'm on my way.'

Thank you for reading my book, I hope you enjoyed it. If you did, would you please be kind enough to leave a favourable review so others can make an informed choice and hopefully enjoy it too.

Many thanks.
Michael

Printed in Great Britain
by Amazon

78183202R00159